Dog's Waiting Room
a golden retriever mystery

Neil S. Plakcy

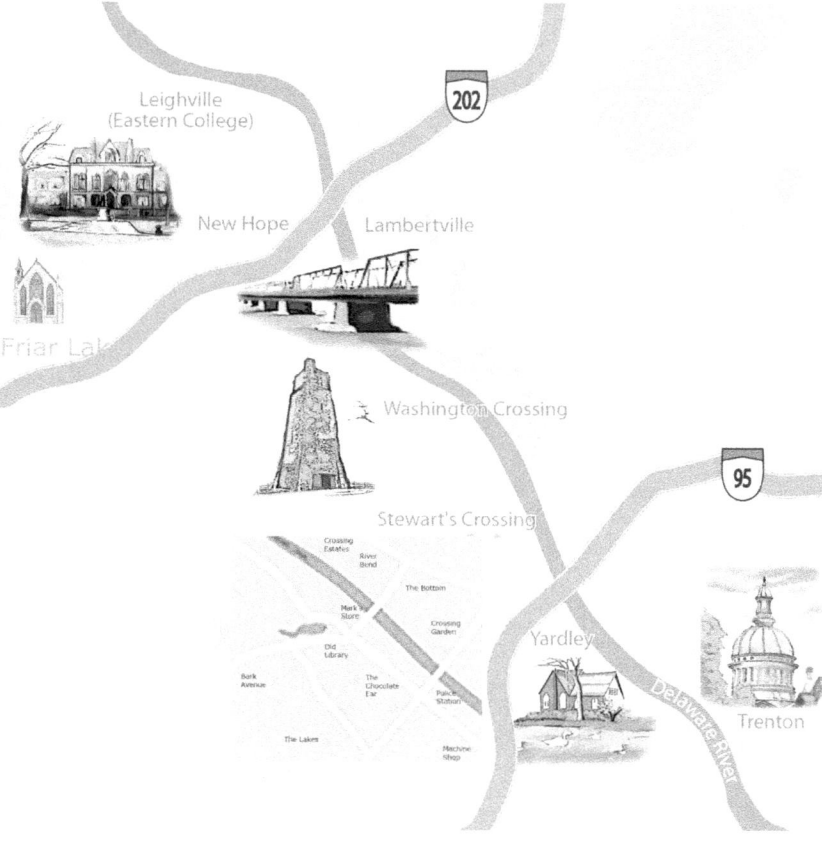

Reviews

Mr. Plakcy did a terrific job in this cozy mystery. He has a smooth writing style that kept the story flowing evenly. The dialogue and descriptions were right on target.

Book Blogger Red Adept

Steve and Rochester become quite a team and Neil Plakcy is the kind of writer that I want to tell me this story. It's a fun read which will keep you turning pages very quickly.

Amos Lassen – *Amazon top 100 reviewer Amos Lassen*

In Dog We Trust is a very well-crafted mystery that kept me guessing up until Steve figured out where things were going.

E-book addict reviews

Neil Plakcy's *Kingdom of Dog* is supposed to be about the former computer hacker, now college professor, Steve Levitan, but it is his golden retriever Rochester who is the real amateur sleuth in this delightful academic mystery. This is no talking dog book, though. Rochester doesn't need anything more than his wagging tail and doggy smile to win over readers and help solve crimes. I absolutely fell in love with this brilliant dog who digs up clues and points the silly humans towards the evidence.

– Christine Kling, author of *Circle of Bones*.

Copyright 2021 Neil S. Plakcy. This cozy mystery is a work of fiction. Names, characters, places, and incidents either are products of the author's imagination or are used fictitiously. Any resemblance to actual events or locales or persons, living or dead, is entirely coincidental.

All rights reserved, including the right of reproduction in whole or in part in any form. Cover by Kelly Nichols; editing by Randall Klein.

Chapter 1
Getting Old is No Picnic

To escape the June heat, I took my golden retriever Rochester for a walk along the Delaware River, a few miles from our townhouse. A narrow path threaded between the River Road and the water's edge, shaded by maples and willows, and it was cool and green there, with plenty of wonderful smells for him to investigate.

We parked, and I let Rochester off his leash. He was a smart dog, savvy enough to keep away from the road and trained enough to come back when I called him. Even so, he generally stayed within a few feet of me as we strolled along the dappled path.

I was so accustomed to seeing Rochester up close that it was a different experience seeing him a few feet away from me. As he walked, I reflected on what a handsome dog he was. with a square head and big brown eyes. His hair was a rich gold that glowed in the light. When I looked up photos of the breed standard online, it was as if Rochester had posed for the pictures himself.

Up ahead of us, I spied an elderly man, white-haired and fragile, and I worried that he might be frightened by a big happy dog. I called Rochester to me, but instead he hurried forward to the man, going down on his front paws in his play position.

The man smiled at him and said something, but I was too far

away to hear. As I got closer, I saw the man bend down and offer his hand to Rochester to sniff. Then he brushed his hand across the soft fur on top of the golden's head.

"Good afternoon," I said as I approached. "I see you've met Rochester. I'm Steve."

"Pleased to meet you. My name is…" He stopped. "I guess it's escaped me for the moment."

That was worrying. "Is there someone with you?" I asked.

"No, I like to go out for my morning constitutional on my own."

It was three o'clock in the afternoon by then. Had this man been out since the morning? Or was he simply as confused about time as he was about his own name?

"Do you live around here?" I asked, though there were no houses close by. An old, old cemetery was across the road from us, with fields on either side of it.

"Oh yes, just down the way. I suppose I should get back there."

My own father had passed away years before, but I hoped that if he had been wandering lost that someone would have helped him. "Can we walk with you?" I asked.

He frowned. "I wouldn't mind the company. But I'm not sure of the direction."

Rochester stopped by my side and squatted on the dry ground. Then he sniffed my pocket, and I realized he knew, too, that this old man was in trouble. I pulled my cell phone out of that pocket and hit the speed dial for my friend Rick Stemper, a detective in the Stewart's Crossing police department.

While the old man petted Rochester, I turned away so he couldn't hear my conversation. "What's up?" Rick asked. "You're still coming over for the barbecue tonight, aren't you?"

"Absolutely." When Rick married his girlfriend Tamsen, he sold the home he'd bought from his parents and moved in with her, in a big house with a fancy grill in the back yard. He had turned into quite the suburban dad, grilling often, and he had invited Lili and me over for ribs and beer. "I have a question, though."

I told him about the old man. "He seems confused. Is there someone I can call to help him find his way home?"

"Call the police non-emergency number," he said. "They'll send a patrol car out to talk to him."

"Will do." I called and told the dispatcher what was going on and agreed to meet a car at the layby on River Road. Then I asked the old man to accompany us back to my car.

As we walked, he said, "I always lived across the river, in Trenton, but I never took the time to come down and walk by the water. I was a busy man."

"What did you do for a living?"

"Property," he said, without thinking about it. "I used to own property all over town. State Street, Prospect Street, all around the Battle Monument."

I'd been born in Trenton, had traveled throughout it during my childhood. State Street was tree-lined, with cobblestone sidewalks, right by the bridge across the river. Our dentist was in the Carteret Arms building there, and after every checkup or filling we'd stop for a slice of chocolate cream pie at the Toddle House.

My mother's cousin lived a few blocks away, in a two-story Colonial a block from the Delaware. After a stop there, we'd head inland past the big stone houses with their broad front porches overlooking Prospect Street to the Polish neighborhood around the Battle Monument, where we'd buy brisket and stuffed cabbage.

"How about you?" he asked. "You grow up in Trenton?"

"For a couple of years. I was born at St. Francis Hospital and my parents lived a few blocks away, on Greenwood Avenue. But then we moved to Stewart's Crossing when I was two."

"All gone now," the man told me. "Everything sold. Except the house where I raised my family, beside Cadwalader Park."

My father had sold our family home after my mother's death, so I knew what it was like to lose a house that meant something. "My mother used to take me to the monkey house at the park," I said. "I hope you didn't live in that direction. It smelled!"

"Oh, yes, it did," he said. "I used to send my kids to play in the park, and I could smell it on them if they'd been near the monkeys." He smiled, and his eyes crinkled. "'Into the bath!' I used to say. "'My children are not monkeys!' Sometimes they wanted me to chase them around, and I did. I was quite the athlete back then. Ran track at Trenton High, then again at Rutgers."

He stopped walking for a moment, as if he had called up a memory he wanted to explore. "My oldest son was a runner, too. But then he got fat and angry. Even a few years ago I was hiking until he made me stop. I tried to tell him that I wasn't like him, that I was still fit, but he wouldn't have it. Said it wasn't my body, but my mind that was going."

He sighed. "I guess he was right. I live with him now," he said. "Oh, yes. Now he's the one who bosses me around. He'll come and get me if I call him. He put his number in my phone." He patted his pockets. "Oh. I must have gone off without it. Jeffrey won't be happy."

"Your son's name is Jeffrey?" That was at least a start for the patrol officer.

"Yes, Jeffrey Lalor." He cocked his head. "Oh. So that must be my name, too. Lalor."

"Like the street in Trenton?" I asked. "Lalor Street?"

He nodded. "Named after my ancestors. Though I can't remember any of them at the moment."

"It's a pleasure to meet you, Mr. Lalor," I said, and stuck my hand out to shake his.

"The pleasure is all mine," he said.

The river burbled beside us as we walked on the dirt path. Mr. Lalor stumbled once or twice, and I reached out to steady him. I wished that I'd been able to spend more time with my father at the end of his life, but I was in California as his health failed. It had been Father's Day the week before and my girlfriend Lili and I, both fatherless, had avoided any celebration, though my dad had been on my mind a lot.

We walked slowly beneath the canopy of oaks, maples, and weeping willows that ran along the Delaware. Mr. Lalor talked in fits and starts about meeting various mayors of the city, grand openings of new apartment buildings, meetings of the Kiwanis and Elks. Talking to him was like getting a capsule history of the city where I was born, though often the pieces were disjointed. He'd jump from the sound of a wrecking ball slamming into an old house he was having demolished to the memory of his second wife, who died shortly after leaving him two more children.

"It was like an insane asylum sometimes, all those kids," he said. "A lot of mouths to feed and little bodies to put clothes and shoes on. I had to be spry to keep up with all of them. One thing I never could do with them was take them swimming. My mother fell in the Delaware once, when she was a young girl, and after that she had a terrible fear of water. She would never let me learn to swim or go out in a boat. Even today, when I go walking by the river, I make sure to stay well back from the bank."

"Good practice," I said. "The bank here can be slippery sometimes, and there isn't much room between the road and the river."

"None of my kids were fearful that way. There were a couple of little ponds in the park, and then the canal at the edge of it, and the river just beyond. This was back in the 1950s, you understand, before they expanded route 29 into a freeway. Back then you could just hop and skip over the two-lane road and you'd be right at the riverfront. I wanted to make sure none of them would drown if they ever fell in."

Mr. Lalor looked proud of himself. He'd managed to keep his family, however many kids, alive. For a moment he stood up more proudly, and I could see beneath his surface frailty that he had once been an athlete. Though he was skinny, there was still muscle in his arms and legs.

"Course I didn't spend that much time with them. I was always working, cutting deals, putting up buildings. Some of them don't appreciate that."

Mr. Lalor's parenting style sounded a lot like my father's. He worked long hours as an engineer and liked to rest on the weekends. I wasn't a sporty kid, and I don't think he ever came to see me in a school play. My time alone with him had been very limited, though I had vivid memories of rushing out of the house when his Volkswagen bug pulled up in the driveway. When I was young enough, I'd jump into his arms; as I got older, I'd take his briefcase from him and lead him into the house by the hand.

I wondered if Mr. Lalor's kids had acted the same way. "Do you have grandchildren?" I asked.

He frowned for a moment, then nodded. I could see him thinking as he counted on his fingers. "Three of them, that I know of," he said. "I always told my boys that I wanted to be a father-in-law before I was a grandfather."

He laughed. "Not that any of the boys had the spunk to do something like that. They all turned into workaholics, like me. Even the girls are tough."

"How many children do you have?"

His memory seemed to be improving the more he talked to me, like there was some internal greasing of the wheels going on. "Three from my first wife. Jeffrey, Anita and Peter. We used to call them the little Japs, running around like they were kamikaze pilots, pulling at their eyelids and pretending to talk Jap."

Well, that wasn't a politically correct memory, but he was an old man, from another generation. I remembered some of the casual racism my parents used, not because they were prejudiced but because they'd never been taught otherwise.

"Then she died, my wife. Cancer." He started to cough, and I gently patted him on the back until he pulled a cloth handkerchief from his pocket and blew his nose. "Couldn't manage the little hooligans on my own, so I found a widow who'd take us all on. She brought two of her own with her, and then we had two more together."

I did the math. "Wow, seven kids."

"You're telling me. But I had bad luck again, and the second wife died, too, only a couple of years later. I was all at sixes and sevens. I had a business to run and teenagers and babies, too. Not to mention Jane's two, who I never much cared for, but you can't just turn orphaned children out to the wolves."

I remembered a comedy from the 1960s, called *Yours, Mine and Ours*, about that situation. Henry Fonda had ten kids, while Lucille Ball had eight. Though that had worked out well—unlike real life.

"They're all on their own now," Lalor said. "I fed and clothed them and educated them and booted them out."

I wondered if that's the way my father had felt. He and my mother had looked forward to their retirement, joking about how they'd feather their empty nest. Then my mother died, and I was too far away from my dad, and too caught up in my own troubles, to know how he felt about being the only bird left behind.

By the time Mr. Lalor and I reached my car he looked very, very tired, and Rochester was walking slowly beside him, keeping a gentle pressure on his right leg to keep him going. I was glad that we had run into him and were able to help him get back to safety.

The officer was a young blonde woman, and she was kind toward Mr. Lalor. "Let's get you settled in the car, and then I'll find your address," she said. She thanked me for calling, and Rochester and I resumed our walk in the other direction.

We went a few hundred yards and the path died out and Rochester stalled, spending too much time sniffing something. That usually means trouble, especially when he started licking the leaves of a bush. "Licky makes you sicky," I said, tugging at his leash.

He looked up at me, his nose and whiskers twitching, as he let loose a stream. I was stuck there in the bright sunshine waiting for him, and all at once the heat overcame me. I tugged on his leash again when he was finished and said, "Rochester, heel."

Sometimes it works and sometimes it doesn't. That day he was in the mood to agree with me, and we turned around and walked back to the car. When we reached it, I leaned down to unhook his leash, and stroked the golden fur that ran down from his head to his back. It was hot to the touch, and I knew I'd made the right choice to turn us around.

Goldens have a two-layer coat that traps air pockets between them, allowing them to stay warmer in winter and cooler in summer, but I could tell from the way that Rochester leaned toward the air conditioning vents that he was as hot as I was.

"Did you make a new friend today, Rochester?" I asked, as we drove back down River Road toward home.

He smiled at me with his goofy grin. Or maybe he was just opening his mouth to let lots of cool air in. Dogs can be mysterious like that. Every now and then I'll be sitting with him, stroking his fur, and his mouth will be closed, giving him a moody look. I'll pull up the edges of his lips and tell him to smile, but usually he resists and simply rolls over.

Sometimes the love between dad and dog can be as mysterious as that between father and son. As Rochester sat up beside me, enjoying the air, I thought again of my father, and though I felt he'd been taken from me too soon I was glad that he hadn't lived to experience the kind of dementia Mr. Lalor demonstrated.

My father had always been the smartest guy in the room. He had served in the Navy during the tail end of World War II, and because he scored so highly on the military IQ test, they'd slotted him immediately into military intelligence. He had never spoken much about what he did, but from what I understood he'd been stationed in Washington DC, evaluating captured German technology and writing reports about it.

I remember being stunned once, sometime while I was in graduate school at Columbia University, when he told me he thought I was smarter than he was. I had poo-pooed it at the time, telling him I simply had more opportunities than he had—which was thanks to him and his hard work.

I hoped that Mr. Lalor's kids appreciated all that he had done for them, the way I appreciated my dad.

Chapter 2
Barbecue

I was pleased when I got home to discover that Lili had made a pitcher of lemonade with fresh lemons, mint leaves, and club soda, the way her mother had learned in Cuba and passed on to her. I had poured myself a big glass when she came into the kitchen and caught me. "That's for tonight!" she said, taking the pitcher from me.

She smiled. "Fortunately, I have some extra lemons and another bottle of club soda. But no more until we get to Tamsen's house."

I considered myself exceedingly lucky that I had convinced Lili to fall for me. I am only average in looks, though every now and then she'll smile and me and tell me I am *"que guapo,"* or handsome in Spanish. She, on the other hand, is a show-stopper, with brown eyes flecked with green, and dark brown curls that show a hint of auburn in the sunlight. She often wears her hair up in a high ponytail, as she did that day, with stray curls framing her heart-shaped face.

Like me, she came from Ashkenazi Jewish stock, though her grandparents had emigrated to Cuba early in the twentieth century and both her parents had been born there. She called herself a Juban, a Jewish Cuban, and she had a Latina liveliness that surfaced most when she laughed and when she danced.

She and I spent the afternoon reading while Rochester snoozed by my feet, and around six o'clock we drove over to Tamsen's house on the other side of town.

Rick was already outside sweating by the barbecue, and I brought him a fresh cold beer. He was the same age as I was, in our mid-forties, and we'd been classmates at Pennsbury High years before. He was trimmer than I was, since I carried a few more pounds than I should, but his hair had more gray in it than mine. We hadn't been close in high school, but when I moved back to Stewart's Crossing we'd reconnected and become best friends.

"What happened with your old man?" he asked.

I shrugged. "Last I saw of him he was in the back seat of a police cruiser. At least he remembered his son's name by then."

"I hope we don't end up like that," he said. "Forgetting everything that matters."

"Sometimes forgetting is better."

Rick and I had bonded back in the day over our bitter divorces. Since then, we had both moved on, and I really liked Tamsen. She was a few years younger than we were, and Rick had met her when he coached her son Justin's Pop Warner football team.

Rick waved his hand around to encompass his Australian Shepherd Rascal playing with Rochester, Justin climbing on his jungle gym, and Lili and Tamsen, sitting across from one another at the picnic table. Lili was dark where Tamsen was fair, but they wore similar short-sleeved shirts and shorts, and they'd become close friends as we had encompassed Tamsen into our circle. "I don't want to forget any of this," he said.

The aroma of the ribs on the barbecue rose up as a warm breeze swept over us. "And I certainly don't want to forget those ribs."

"It was interesting," I said, as we waited for the ribs to cook. "Here's this old guy, and he can't remember his name at first, but as we got to talking he remembered bits and pieces of his life. But he wasn't angry about it or depressed. He was just happy to be in the moment, walking along the river in the sunlight and the shade. He talked about his kids, and the monkey house at Cadwalader Park, and how he built buildings around Trenton and provided for his family."

"That's what all of us want, isn't it?" Rick asked. "To remember the good times. To feel like we took care of the people who matter to us."

"Is that all, though? Sometimes I wonder if I've done anything that really matters in the world. No kids to raise. I haven't cured cancer or run for office or done anything that could leave my mark." I leaned back against the house, my beer dampening my hands. "At least you, you're a cop. You save lives and make the world a safer place."

He laughed. "Usually I fill out paperwork and arrest people for breaking and entering or spraying graffiti. Not exactly saving the world."

He flipped one set of ribs. "But you've done good in your own way. You've help bring criminals to justice. Solved a couple of mysterious crimes." He looked at me. "There are people who feel better, who've gotten closure over the death of a loved one, because of what you've done."

"I know. I'm just feeling melancholy after hearing Mr. Lalor brag about all his achievements."

"I guarantee the guy has a dark side," Rick said. "We all do. We just don't choose to present that to people. Look at you and your hacking. You did some stuff that society considers wrong, and you paid the price for it. But it probably won't be something you go blabbing about to strangers when you turn eighty."

"I guess not. Maybe it's that we had Father's Day last weekend and I didn't have my dad to celebrate with, and I've connected Mr. Lalor with him."

"Justin made me a card and drew footballs all over it. He wrote that he was glad I was his dad because now I'd have to keep being his Pop Warner coach."

"Sweet," I said, and I felt a pang of regret that I'd never get a card like that.

"I called my father in Florida to wish him Happy Father's Day. And you know what? My mom said he was out on the golf course and he'd get back to me. But that they were going out to dinner with friends and they'd probably go to bed as soon as they got home, so not to wait for a call."

"And did he ever call you?"

Rick shook his head. "I call my mom every couple of days, just to check on her and my dad. Like three days later, when I hadn't heard from him, I called, and she put him on the phone. And you know what he said?"

"What?"

"I said, 'Happy Father's Day, Pop,' and he said, 'ah, that's yesterday's news. What have you got for me today?'"

I laughed, though it had to have hurt Rick's feelings. "What did you say to that?"

"I said, that's what I'll put on your tombstone, Pop. Yesterday's news." He smiled. "He went off on this tirade about how expensive funerals are these days. Apparently, he and my mom are looking into pre-need arrangements, even though there's nothing wrong with either of them, as far as I know. He said he'd be just as happy with a pine box, but my mother wants a more extravagant package."

"Parents," I said. "You can't live with them, and you can't kill them. And if you do, you have to figure out what to do with the bodies."

As Rick served up the ribs, I noticed Rochester at the edge of Tamsen's property, digging at the base of a tree. Usually he's first in line when there's food on the table, so I hurried over to see what he was doing. As I arrived, he sat back on his hind legs and barked once.

In the shady light filtering through the tree branches, I caught a glint of gold. I looked down and spotted a broken chain with a gold locket still attached. I picked it up and carried it back to the table. "Look what Rochester found," I said, as I held it up. "I guess he's going into the gold mining business on the side. Unless this is a clue to something?"

My crime-solving dog had a reputation for sniffing out clues, using his exquisite sense of smell and his ability to connect with humans, or to know when one of them wasn't acting correctly.

"My locket!" Tamsen said, and I handed it to her. "Justin climbed up that tree the other day and then he was afraid to climb down, so I had him jump and I caught him. That night when I went to take my jewelry off, I realized it was gone."

She opened the locket and showed us the pictures. Her late husband Ryan, who had died a war hero in Afghanistan, was on one side, and a baby picture of Justin on the other. "I thought it was a message, that it was time to put this away."

Lili put her hand on Tamsen's arm. "At least you have it back now."

Tamsen smiled. "And I know just the pictures I'm putting in. A head shot of Rick from our wedding, and Justin's last school picture."

Justin stuck out his tongue. "Not that one, Mom. That looks so fake."

Rick said, "Who knows, Sport, maybe that's the way your mom wants to remember you. Fake you, not real you."

"Da-ad," Justin said, and then he picked up a rib and started chewing on it.

Ryan had died before Justin could form any real memories of him, and until Rick and Tamsen got married, he'd called Rick "Coach," because that's how they had met, over football. As soon as Rick proposed to Tamsen, Justin had asked if he could call Rick "Dad."

Rick, of course, had agreed, leaving both him and me misty-eyed.

We ate, we talked, we laughed, and the dogs played with Justin. Rascal's natural instinct was to herd, and it was funny to see him running alongside Rochester, nipping at him or barking when he wanted my dog to turn. I know I spoiled the golden too much and it was fun to see him get bossed around.

It was a mellow summer evening, with lightning bugs coming out after dark. Rick and I tried to help Justin catch one in a glass jar, but without success. Some things are destined to run free.

We returned late that evening to our townhouse in River Bend, a gated community at the north end of Stewart's Crossing, and I took Rochester for a quick walk.

When we got back to the house, I heard Lili's raised voice coming from upstairs, and realized that she was speaking rapid, almost angry Spanish. She had grown up with the language, and it still flavored her speech, though I rarely heard her speak it with such fluency and passion.

Her voice grew louder as she descended the stairs. *"Adiós Fedi. Te hablaré mañana."*

"Your brother?" I asked, as she walked into the kitchen, her cell phone in her hand. She had pinned her exuberant auburn curls up against her head, but a few strands had fallen out. I had the urge to put them back in place, but Lili was too agitated.

"My mother called Fedi this morning because she wanted him to hire an aide for her. You've heard me talk about her enough to know that's a huge red flag—she's resisted having anyone in the apartment with her for ages."

She stopped to take a breath. "He finally wormed it out of her that she had fallen so he rushed over there and she admitted that her hip hurt. Fedi called 911 and they took her right to the hospital. She fractured her right hip and they're going to have to replace it."

Lili's brother Federico, aka Fedi, lived in a suburb of Fort Lauderdale with his wife and two children. Fedi had added a mother-in-law unit to his house, but their mother refused to leave her oceanfront apartment, even though she was having more and more difficulty living on her own.

"Oh my," I said. "The poor woman."

"I have to get there right away. If I can find a flight tomorrow morning, can you drive me to the airport?"

Lili was more agitated than I'd ever seen her. "Of course. But come here for a minute."

"What?"

"Just come here." I patted the sofa next to me. She came over and sat down beside me, and I pulled her close. She rested her head against my shoulder.

"I knew this was going to happen someday, but it still... I don't know. I can't process it."

"Your mother has always been a rock," I said. "You've had her to turn to whenever you've had a crisis in your life. But I want you to know that I can be your rock."

She put her hand on my knee. "I know, sweetheart. And I appreciate it. It's just a hard transition. She's going to need help, and she's going to resist every step of the way."

She sat up. "This is her payback, for all the grief I gave her when I married Philip, and then divorced him, and then married and divorced Adriano. I know that it tore her heart out to see me unhappy." She stood up. "And now I know how she felt."

Lili was busy for the next hour arranging her flight, a rental car, and talking to both her mother and Fedi. The surgery was scheduled for Monday afternoon, which gave Lili plenty of time to get there, see her mother and talk to her before she went under.

"I feel terrible that this whole burden has fallen on Fedi and Sara," Lili said, as she sat beside me on the couch. "But I don't know what else to do. My mother would hate it up here, and I can't give up my job, and expect you to give up yours, and move us all down to Florida."

"I could be a kept man," I said. "If you found a job in a warmer climate. God knows I'm not eager to face another Pennsylvania winter. You're a Latina, you speak Spanish. Couldn't you get a job down there somewhere?"

Since meeting Lili, I'd learned the fine distinction that governed her background. Because her family did not trace back to Spain, as so many Central and South Americans did, she wasn't Hispanic. But she had been born in Cuba to Cuban-born parents, so that made her a bona fide Latina.

"You'd really pick up and move? Leave behind everything you've built here?"

"To make you happy? In a heartbeat."

"That's so sweet of you." She cocked her head and looked at me for a moment, and I could see the wheels turning in her brain. "But two weeks around my mother will be all I can take, with her criticizing me and everything I've done."

"I wish she could see you the way I do," I said. "The amazing photos you've taken, the awards you've won for your photojournalism, the good person you are."

"You're sweet. And I know she'll love you. A nice Jewish boy."

"With a criminal record."

"She doesn't know about that," Lili said. "Is that a problem for you?"

"Not at all. I've done my best to put that all behind me, and though I'm never going to hide my past, it doesn't have to define me."

Lili and I had both tried to move on from difficult times. She had spent years as a globe-trotting photojournalist and part of the appeal of that career had been that it kept her from dwelling too long on her failed marriages and whatever else plagued her.

We had met soon after she joined Eastern College as chair of the Fine Arts faculty. I believed that settling down with me was easing those pains.

Rochester rose from the floor and nuzzled my leg, and while I scratched behind his ears, Lili stroked his flanks. I'd read somewhere that petting a dog had physical effects like reducing your heart rate and raising your endorphin levels, and I believed it.

I hoped that stroking him would relax Lili, too, and help her push away some of the stress of worrying about her mother.

Chapter 3
The Way Women Talk

Lili went upstairs to call some cousins, and I stayed on the living room floor with Rochester. The fine hair beside his ears, which reminded me of the *payess* worn by Orthodox Jews, had become tangled, and I got the special comb I'd bought and began to tease the strands clear.

I combed out tangles and then moved on to the rest of his eighty-pound body and pulled off wads of loose fur. He was a sweet boy but he shed like a monster, and each brushing accumulated enough golden threads to knit a sweater. As I combed him, I thought about my own parents.

I was sorry that they had never been able to meet Lili. They didn't care for my ex-wife, Mary. But my mother had kept her mouth shut—I'd brought home a Jewish girl, after all, one who was smart and pretty and career-oriented like her, and that was a lot better than many of the sons of her friends and cousins, and she wasn't one to tempt fate by complaining.

My father, on the other hand, had made it clear in small ways that he thought Mary was too bossy, too sharp-tongued. "You need a wife who will treat you like an equal," he had said to me several times. "That woman talks to you like you work for her."

"It's a relationship, Dad," I'd said. "Modern women work twice as hard to succeed as men do, and sometimes Mary has a hard time leaving that attitude behind at the office."

He had only snorted. By the time Mary and I divorced, my mother had passed away and he was already suffering from the cancer that would kill him. I was locked up in California then, serving a year's sentence for hacking into the three major credit bureaus to prevent Mary from bankrupting us after her second miscarriage. Our brief phone calls centered around his health, though I could tell he was happy that Mary had moved on.

What would he think of Lili? He'd always appreciated a beautiful woman, and with her curvaceous figure, flashing dark eyes and heart-shaped face, Lili radiated beauty. She also had a kindness that Mary lacked, that I was sure he'd have responded well to.

The dog with me woofed gently, and I looked down at him. I had a plastic grocery bag full of hair, and Rochester rolled onto his back and waved his legs in the air like a dying cockroach. That was his sign that he wanted his belly rubbed.

I complied, as I always did.

The next time Lili came downstairs she said, "Am I making a terrible mistake by going to Florida? My mother gets angry every time she sees me. I'm afraid I'll only agitate her more by being there."

I had spoken to Señora Weinstock a couple of times on the phone. "*Al fin un Judío,*" she had said to me in our initial conversation. At last, Lili had found a Jew. According to Lili, her mother had never approved of either of her two ex-husbands – though in retrospect, she admitted, her mother might have been right.

Señora Weinstock seemed to have a lot of Lili's fire and determination, though underlaid with a sense that the world was against her—conspiring to chase her from her childhood home and leave her to roam the earth unmoored. What would she think of me, a man with a checkered past, too old to give her more grandchildren, not wealthy enough to provide her daughter with the life she deserved?

Lili sat on the sofa next to me, where she rested her head on my shoulder. "What if I lose her?" she asked.

"You will, someday," I said. "Try to have as few regrets as possible when that happens."

"Which means yes, I need to go to Florida."

"Yup. And you need to think about her, not yourself."

She sat up and turned towards me. "Excuse me?"

"If she irritates you, don't bite back. She's in pain, and she's had a lifetime of trouble, from what you've told me. So focus on what you can do to help her. If she needs to vent, be her audience, even if she says hurtful things. That's the best way you can show her love."

"How did you get so smart?"

"It's all thanks to Rochester." I reached down to pat the fine hairs on the top of his head. "Isn't that right, boy?"

He woofed and looked up at me, and the love in those big brown eyes was almost overwhelming. What a lucky guy I was, to have Lili and Rochester beside me on this trip around the sun.

Monday morning, light was beginning to dawn in the east as I drove Lili down I-95 to the airport in Philadelphia, with Rochester in the back, squeezed between suitcases. I pulled up in the drop-off lane exactly an hour before her flight was due to leave. I kissed her goodbye and told her to call me whenever she needed to vent.

"Be prepared for frequent calls." She reached behind her and scratched beneath Rochester's chin. "Take care of your daddy, boy."

He leaned forward and rested his head on my shoulder, and as soon as Lili was out of the car, he scrambled into the front seat beside me. While we waited at a traffic light, I reached over and hooked his harness. I got right back onto I-95 and since a breeze blew through along the highway, I lowered the windows and Rochester stuck his head out. The wind pulled the hair on his head and his mane back, accentuating his noble profile.

"It's just you and me for the next few days," I said to him as we rolled past tractor-trailers, company vans, and big honking SUVs that were almost as large as RVs. "Anything special you want to do?"

He looked back at me for a moment and grinned, then returned to the open window. "I guess that means I get to make the choices," I said. "I'm thinking long walks and lots of belly rubs. Hope that works for you."

He didn't respond, just strained forward so far to catch passing smells that I felt obliged to tug back on his harness so he didn't go flying out onto the highway.

I followed I-95 until it connected with I-295, which led me to the Yardley exit. Since I was already inland, I took Taylorsville Road north. Almost immediately we passed a big empty space between woods where there had once been a model train track with kid-sized cars, run by a genial older man.

Where there once had been endless fields and undeveloped woodlands, now suburban developments had sprung up like mushrooms. I wondered if old Mr. Lalor was responsible for any of it. They all had stone entrance gates and evocative names like Oak Trace and Galloping Run. The trees were all young, many of them held up by wooden braces, and the landscaping around the houses scant. It would take a while for these places to grow into real neighborhoods.

At the town of Potter's Harbor, I turned inland and uphill to Friar Lake, the conference center I managed for Eastern College. It was a collection of buildings of local gray stone on the top of a low hill, with a sparkling lake below us that had recently become part of a county park. An order of Catholic monks had built the complex of buildings, then known as Our Lady of the Waters, over a hundred years before.

My office was in the former gatehouse, and I pulled up in front of it and let Rochester out. As in River Bend, the lawns were a rich green, and Rochester rushed around sniffing and peeing.

My morning was as slow and lazy as an old hound dog in the

summer sun until my phone trilled with the ring tone I had chosen for Lili, Jimmy Buffett's "Jimmy Dreams," the place where he sings about rediscovering his heart.

"How'd your mom do?" I asked, in lieu of a greeting.

"Her heart stopped twice during the surgery," Lili said, choking back tears. "They managed to restart it but she's very weak."

"I'm coming down there," I said. "I don't want you to face this on your own."

"Oh, Steve," she said, and she was crying again, and I was killing myself because I wasn't there to hold her. She had to go back to her mother's side, so I hung up and found online that I could get a flight to Miami that evening. I called Rick and arranged to leave Rochester with him for a few days.

Then the big golden and I walked over to the stone outbuilding where the Friar Lake co-manager, Joey Capodilupo, had his office. Joey handled all the aspects of physical plant, including maintenance and grounds. His work was greater during the summer, as the lawns needed to be mowed more regularly, and he was able to schedule bigger jobs without worrying about inconveniencing attendees.

He wasn't there, but Rochester put his nose to the ground and quickly tracked him down, supervising a roof repair on the dormitory building. "Lili's in Miami and her mom is sick. I want to go there tonight for a few days. Can you hold the fort?"

"Of course."

We took a few minutes to hash out the rest of the week, which involved him accepting a delivery of printed flyers for upcoming events, and not much else. Then I drove home. The BMW was too old to have a Bluetooth connection for my phone, so as we drove I usually fed through a series of CDs, sharing my musical tastes with Rochester. He liked Bruce Springsteen and Southside Johnny, but when I plugged in the original cast album for *Pump Boys and Dinettes*, he rolled over and put his paw over his ear.

I didn't care, singing along with "No holds barred, baby, I'm going to Florida. Won't you come along with me."

Rochester alternated between sitting up to peer out the window or slumping down on the seat with his head resting on my knee. He clearly knew something was wrong.

Back at River Bend, I packed quickly, and bagged up Rochester's food and a couple of toys. No grilling of burgers that night.

Then we drove over to Tamsen and Rick's. Instead of jumping out like he usually did as soon as I pulled to a stop and opened the door for him, he sat on the seat and stared at me.

"Come on, puppy, you love visiting Rascal. You two can play all day."

From inside the house, he heard his friend's bark, and answered with a yip of his own. Then with one last baleful glance at me, he jumped out of the car and rushed up to the front door.

After a few kisses—for Rochester, not for Rick – I left for the airport, and was able to park in a long-term lot and take the shuttle to the terminal. I even made it to the gate with a few minutes to spare. Enough time to share a quick call with Lili and reassure her that I was on my way.

Lili had a rental car, and she had promised to pick me up at the airport, so after the flight and a flurry of text messages I found myself walking through the heat and fumes of the covered drop-off lanes of Miami International Airport, dodging rent-a-car minivans and cruising taxis.

A dark-skinned woman in a nurse's uniform aggressively shook a white can filled with change at me as I passed a quartet of French Canadians arguing with each other over the best way to get to Hollywood.

I had heard a lot about Miami but never visited. I wondered if any of the people around me were Colombian drug couriers with cocaine-filled condoms in their bowels who sweated and looked forward to toilets in safe houses, or which of the men with oversized suitcases were carrying illegal birds or reptiles.

A KIA Soul beeped several times at me, and I realized it was Lili at the wheel. I tossed my bag into the back seat and jumped into the front with her. As she navigated us past a construction project on one of the garages, a cab driver tried to cut her off, but she lowered her window and yelled at him, "*¡Me cago en la boca de tu madre!*"

"What in the world does that mean?"

"I shit in your mother's mouth," she said, conversationally. "Hey, we're in Miami. Got to act like a native."

Two lanes of the highway were closed for a road construction project, and in the last of the day's sunlight the chunks of torn asphalt gleamed in the heat like black diamonds. In the distance, a wavering curtain of steam seemed to rise from the pavement.

Toto, we're not in Pennsylvania anymore, I thought.

Chapter 4
Clearing a Path

Lili waited until we were out of the airport and on a highway with the setting sun at our back to fill me in. "It's chaos here. My mother is very agitated. She keeps pulling her oxygen mask off and she rambles in a weird combination of Spanish and Yiddish. I have no idea what she's saying most of the time."

"Sounds terrible. Where are Fedi and Sara while this is happening?"

"They're worn out, so it's all on me right now."

I felt bad for Lili, and guilty at the same time. I hadn't been able to be there for either of my parents as their health declined, and I wouldn't do or say anything to put Lili in the same situation.

"I am totally overwhelmed," she said. "I'm talking to the doctors and nurses whenever I can, and trying to find her a place to go for rehab. Not to mention refereeing arguments between her and Fedi."

"What can I do to help?"

"Just having you here is helping already. I want to spend as much time as I can with my mother and talking to her doctors. Fedi and I have agreed that she's never going to be able to go back to the condo, and it's going to take a huge effort to clean it up. Do you think you could get started on that tomorrow?"

"Absolutely."

"It won't all be horrible, I promise. The view from the apartment is spectacular and there's a terrace where we can have a glass of wine. There's a pool and a beach."

"It'll be fine," I said. "As long as we're together."

It was fully dark by the time we turned onto a causeway over to Sunny Isles Beach, where Lili's mother had bought a condo soon after becoming a widow. The long commercial street that led east from the highway was fascinating, a mix of Chinese groceries, Jamaican restaurants, and payday lenders, lined with towering palm trees. Even on a Monday evening the traffic was heavy.

The bridge over the Intracoastal was going up and we came to a stop on the approach ramp, with an amazing view south along the water toward the high-rise towers of downtown Miami. Bells rang on the bridge, and the air was fresh with a hint of saltwater. Gorgeous. It was hard to believe I'd woken up that morning in my townhouse in Stewart's Crossing, where the only exotic thing was the way the developer had named all the streets after cities in eastern Europe.

The expensive yacht finally completed its transit beneath us, and the bridge closed. Lili turned left on Collins Avenue, and a couple of blocks later, pulled into the driveway of a high-rise that fronted on the ocean. She pressed a button on the side wall, spoke to a disembodied voice, and a metal grille swung open. Since her mother no longer had a car, we parked in her space in the low, dim garage.

"Brace yourself," Lili said as we rode up in the elevator. "My mother's apartment looks like one of those hoarder TV shows."

She exaggerated, but not by much. The apartment, which was spacious and looked out at the ocean, would have been lovely except for the fact that her mother was a pack rat.

There was stuff everywhere. Table lamps, collectibles, piles of newspapers, manila and accordion folders of paperwork. The étagère was crowded with framed photos of Lili, her brother and sister-in-law, and the grandkids.

"This is beautiful," I said, waving my arm. "How does your mother feel about not coming back here?"

"We haven't told her." She shook her head. "*Dios mio.* She's a pill. But when we were sick as kids, she always used to say *Di tsayt iz der bester dokter.* Time is the best doctor. We'll give her time to get better and then spring it on her."

"How do you do that?" I asked. "Jump around between Spanish and English and Yiddish?"

She shrugged. "Whatever sounds right," she said. "Spend some time in Miami, you'll understand. We'll have you speaking Spanglish in no time."

We stepped out onto the terrace. "This building is way nicer than I expected," I said. "From the way you talked I was figuring on one of those catwalk buildings filled with old people watching to see who went out in the ambulance next."

"My parents were misers," she said. "They never spent a penny they didn't have to, so they built up a lot of savings. After my father died, my mother decided she was going to change her ways, and that she wanted to live by the beach. Up until recently she was swimming every day." She turned to me. "You brought a bathing suit, didn't you?"

"I did, though I wasn't sure we'd have a chance to swim."

"I want to swim every morning. It kept my mother young for years."

I'd never known that Lili liked to swim, or that her parents had been wealthy enough to afford such a luxurious condo. She led me on a tour; the master bedroom terrace connected to the one for the living room and from the bed you could see the vast expanse of the Atlantic. Señora Weinstock had used the second bedroom as an office, and Lili pointed out how jammed the shelves and file cabinets were.

"I wanted to start cleaning up, but by the time I got back from the hospital I was too exhausted," she said. "Whatever you can do would be a help."

"No problem," I said, and my old impulse to snoop reared its head. I'd enjoy looking at snippets of Lili's family past.

Lili had been raiding her mother's freezer, which was filled with individual-sized plastic containers. "My mother never got accustomed to cooking for one," she said, as she browsed through the offerings. "She figured out she could make her big dishes and then freeze them in portions. You have a choice of *ropa vieja*, *picadillo*, or lentil stew."

"I'll pass on the lentils," I said. "How's her *picadillo*? Does she make the ground beef with raisins and potatoes like you do?"

"Where do you think I learned?"

"I'm sure yours is better, but I'll give hers a try."

"You are very diplomatic, Mr. Levitan," she said. "Be sure to use that charm on my mother. Maybe you can get her to smile once she wakes up."

As she warmed up *ropa vieja* for herself and *picadillo* for me, I moved our bags from the foyer into the master bedroom. After I tasted both dishes I could honestly say I liked the way Lili cooked better. "That's just because these have been frozen and reheated," she said. "My mother is twice the cook I'll ever be."

"Let's hope she's twice the hoarder you'll ever be, too," I said, looking around. The kitchen was jammed with old and new appliances on the counter, including a huge wooden mixing bowl with a heavy stone club and what looked like one of the first microwave ovens ever made. Every available space on the wall was filled with illustrations of tropical fruits.

"Fortunately, that gene skipped me," Lili said. "The only thing I'm going to keep collecting is art."

Perhaps in reaction to her mother, Lili was the opposite of a pack rat—she tossed every piece of mail, sometimes even things that needed to be answered. She religiously weeded through her closet, donating clothes that she hadn't worn in the last year, and she prided herself on her ability to pack for a round-the-world trip in under fifteen minutes.

I wasn't so thorough myself, and I had accumulated a collection of golden retriever knickknacks that I'd never part with—signs that proclaimed my dog was smarter than an honors student, to beware of being licked to death and so on. I loved Rochester, so sue me.

It was good to fall asleep with Lili beside me, and I'd have been happy to sleep in Tuesday morning, but Lili wanted to swim, and then get over to the hospital early to catch her mother's doctors on their morning rounds.

We pulled on our bathing suits and took the elevator down to the beach behind the condo. The water was cooler than I expected, and I had to plunge in all at once to get over it. We swam lazily together for a while. I could get used to this kind of life.

Then she wanted to get moving, so we went upstairs and after showers and a brief breakfast, she left and I got started on the stacks of newspapers her mother had collected. I found a recycling bin beside the trash chute, and I filled it with paper. There was still a lot more to get rid of, but I'd wait until someone emptied the bin before filling it again.

Señora Weinstock had a small copier, and it looked like she had taken each bill, photocopied it, then copied her check and stapled it all together, along with the envelope the bill had come in and whatever junk had come with it. I found a staple remover on the kitchen table and began going through the pages.

My stomach began to grumble during the afternoon and I looked in the refrigerator, which was jammed with bottles and jars and plastic containers that were nearly empty. An inch of orange juice in one bottle, a few dregs of guava jam in a jar, and so on. At least nothing was rotten, though a couple of tomatoes were well past their sell-by date.

I cobbled together a quick lunch of leftovers and filled a trash bag with empties. I could see why Lili hadn't wanted to get started on this job—wherever I looked there was more to do.

Lili came home around five that evening and looked around the living room. "Wow! You've made a ton of progress."

Yeah, I'd gotten rid of a couple of stacks of newspaper and cleared a path to the coffee table, but all I saw was how much more there was to do. "I'm just focusing on trash right now," I said. "I'm going to need your help once I get down a couple of layers to things that you might want to keep."

"You make it sound like Pompeii after Vesuvius. A couple of layers."

"Yeah, well Mount Benita exploded in here," I said. "I'm just the archaeologist combing through the debris."

She laughed and put her arm in mine, and we walked to a Cuban restaurant a couple of blocks away. Lili ordered for us in Spanish, and she seemed so comfortable in Florida, after only a few days. Was this where she belonged, in a place where her Jewish, Cuban, and American strands could all come together into a shiny braid like the one she sometimes pulled her auburn curls into?

I was more nervous than I wanted to admit about meeting Lili's mother the next day. A hospital room wasn't the ideal setting for a first encounter, with both of us in unfamiliar surroundings. Lili wasn't vain, but she did like to look her best, and I was sure that was a trait she'd inherited from her mother. What if Lili wasn't able to doll her up enough—would that make her cranky?

What would Señora Weinstock think of me, anyway? Would she press for details about my background, my divorce, my return to Stewart's Crossing? I didn't want to lie about my past but I didn't want her to think badly of me before she'd even gotten to know me.

Chapter 5
Royal Audience

While we were eating, Rick texted that Rochester was fine, eating well and playing with Rascal, so at least that was one worry I could shelve.

The next morning we swam again, and Lili left to get her mother ready for our meeting. I spent a couple of hours tackling paperwork going back decades, pulling out the occasional thing Lili might like to see – the receipt for rent on her family's first apartment in the United States, a couple of Polaroid photos of her and Fedi as kids and so on.

My phone rang around noon. "She's eating lunch now. Why don't you leave in a few minutes? I dropped a little rum in her coffee so she should be feeling pretty good."

I laughed, but I felt relieved at the same time. I called an Uber, and the driver didn't even need Lili's directions to get me to Mt. Sinai Medical Center, which was a straight run down State Road A1A.

I checked in with the guard on duty, handed over my driver's license and was photographed for a paper badge, then directed to Señora Weinstock's room on the second floor. I knocked on the open door and stuck my head in. Lili sat on the chair beside her mother's bed. Señora Weinstock sat up, looking quite regal, her dark hair teased into a bouffant. Her lips were red and there were touches of blush on her cheeks.

"Steve. Come on in." Lili stood up and as I came toward her she took my hand. "Mamita, this is Steve."

Señora Weinstock smiled, and I leaned down to kiss her cheek. *"Que guapo."*

It was sweet that she thought I was handsome. "My mother will be a hundred years old and she'll still be flirting like a young girl," Lili said.

"From your mouth to God's ears." I backed away from the kiss. "I'm so pleased to meet you," I said to Lili's mother. "I can see where Lili gets her beauty from."

"Tell me about your people," she said, as she motioned me to the chair beside her. "Where are they from?" Her accent wasn't as strong as many I'd heard, but there was a Spanish melody to her speech in the way she accented and pronounced certain words.

"We're all Ashkenazi." I described how each of my grandparents had come to the United States, from various parts of Russia, Lithuania and Belarus.

"And you were a bar mitzvah?"

I smiled. "I was. My Torah portion was about Moses sending men out to explore the territory God was going to give to the Israelites."

"You remember that?" Lili asked.

"I looked it up a while ago. My speech was about exploring new territories and how I was looking forward to high school and college."

Señora Weinstock nodded in approval. "You have a master's degree, Lili says."

"From Columbia University in New York," I said.

"Good. Lili needs a smart, educated man to keep up with her."

"Mami," Lili said.

"What? You think I don't know my own daughter? The world traveler, the college professor? Those other husbands of yours, they wanted you to be the way they wanted. Neither of them saw you for who you are."

She leaned forward. "And you, eh-Steve? What do you see in my daughter?"

I heard her accent in the way she added that extra syllable to my name. My eyes opened wide, but the answer came easily to me. "Lili is all the things you said—she's smart, she's a world traveler, and of course she's beautiful. But I also see how much she cares about her students, what a good heart she has. She makes me want to be as compassionate as she is."

"Steve. You're embarrassing me."

Her mother nodded, though. "When Liliana was a little girl, she was always looking after her brother. Whenever we moved somewhere new, she would make friends first, and then make sure Fedi had friends, too. I'm glad you see that quality in her."

We chatted for a while longer, Lili's mother providing a few embarrassing examples from Lili's childhood which I found charming. And then without warning she said, "I'm tired now. I'm going to take a nap."

"I'll come see you tomorrow," Lili said.

"*Bien*," her mother said. "*Adios, mi amor*."

The royal audience was over. Lili kissed her mother's cheek, and then the two of us walked out of the room. "That went well," I said.

"I knew it would," she said. "What's not to love about you?"

It was my turn to blush.

We went back to the condo, where Lili and I focused on cleaning for a couple of hours. Her brother Fedi was going to stop by the hospital on his way home from work to see his mother, and he'd call with a report on her condition.

So it wasn't a surprise when Lili's phone rang about seven that evening. I was out on the balcony, watching a cruise ship head north to dock at Port Everglades. Lights blazed on all decks, illuminating brightly colored flags and hanging lifeboats.

Lili was on the sofa, looking through a photo album, which she put aside to pick up her phone. "*Hola*, Fedi," she said.

She listened for a moment, then her eyes opened wide, and she began to sob. Deep and gut-wrenching, like an opera diva standing over the body of her slain lover. My heart sped up as I hurried over to her. "What's the matter?"

I had rarely seen Lili cry, and witnessing it now, when she'd been upset for days, caused a feeling to well up inside me, a desire to protect her, to comfort her, to be the knight in shining armor that she had said I'd been in the past for others who had suffered losses.

I sat beside her on the sofa. Her hand was trembling, and her tears were dripping down her cheeks and splashing to her blouse. Through the open balcony door I heard the roar of a powerboat engine and the faint cries of laughter from its passengers.

Lili turned to face me. "My mother," she said, between gulps of air. "She had another heart attack right before Fedi arrived, and they couldn't revive her."

Chapter 6
Nicknames

I put my arm around Lili's shoulders as she spoke to her brother in Spanish so rapid I couldn't follow. When she finally ended the call, she put the phone down and leaned her head on my shoulder. "Fedi has all the papers," she said, almost robotically. "Her pre-need stuff. He'll call the funeral home to pick her up."

She sat up then, turned, and looked at me. She had stopped crying, but I could see the tracks of her tears on her face. "What if something I said this afternoon upset her?"

I shook my head. "I don't believe you did anything wrong. And I don't want to sound cocky, but I think she was glad to know that I was here to take care of you. That she could go when she wanted, on her terms, and know that both you and Fedi have people you love around you."

She pulled a tissue from her pocket and dried her eyes and her cheeks. "That is so New Age-y," she said, with a slight smile. "But that's Benita Weinstock for you. Always on her terms."

She stood up. "I'd like to go for a walk. Will you come with me?"

"Of course. I will live in your heart, die in your lap, and be buried in your eyes—and, what's more, I will walk with you wherever you wish."

She looked at me. "That must be Shakespeare."

I feigned astonishment. "What, I'm not poetical enough for those to be my words?" Then I smiled. "My favorite Shakespeare play is..."

"*Much Ado about Nothing*," she answered promptly. "But it doesn't end like that."

"No, it ends with Benedick agreeing to accompany Beatrice to her uncle's to learn about the perfidy of Don John and the innocence of Hero." I squeezed her hand. "But even though Shakespeare said it first I mean every word of it."

All we had to do was put on beach shoes, and we were out the door of the condo. We rode down in the elevator in silence, then Lili led me out the back door to the wooden staircase that led down to the sand. She leaned down and pulled off her flip-flops and stowed them in her pocket, and I did the same.

The sand was cool underfoot and very loose, though it got more solid the closer we got to the ocean. Lili began walking along the incoming tide, letting the water rush across her toes, and I did the same thing.

"I'm an orphan," she said finally. She turned to me. "How does that feel?"

"Honestly?" I asked. "I don't really feel like I ever lost my parents, because they're in my brain. Every time I do something with my hands, I think of my father and how he lectured me about safety. And when I use a coupon at the grocery I remember my mother. And at weird times I remember Yiddish sayings they taught me."

I turned to her. "Do you remember your father?"

"Of course."

"Because he has a place in your heart, and an even bigger place in your brain. Your parents are never really going to be gone."

"But I won't be able to call her." Her voice twisted on the words.

"Would you like me to complain to you on her behalf? I can. You just have to teach me the Spanish words." I tried to speak in higher voice. "Liliana, *mi hija*, what are you doing with your life? You run so fast from place to place."

She laughed. "Ay, mamita, I have slowed down, now that I have found a man who can keep me grounded, and still let me fly when I need to."

I put my arm in hers. "See, we can act out all those old dramas if you want."

She leaned her head against my shoulder. "I'd rather create new ones. With you."

From down the beach we heard the faint strains of Latin music. Lili stepped away and then took my hand in hers. She began a simple two-step, moving from side to side, and I copied her. Then she added some up-and down movements from her shoulders, and a sexy sway of her hips. I did my best to follow her until the music ended.

"I can do this," she said, squeezing my hand. "With you."

I knew that she didn't mean the dancing.

≈≈≈

We Jews don't like to keep our loved ones around for very long after they die. Because Señora Weinstock had done all the appropriate paperwork in advance, Fedi and Lili were able to schedule the funeral for Thursday. "Morning, Fedi says, because it gets so hot here during the day," Lili told me the next morning, after we had our swim and breakfast, and after a long call with her brother.

"What do you have to do today?"

"I have to take clothes over to the funeral home." She started to cry again. "I wasn't expecting this. She was old and she was going to go eventually, but not now. Not like this."

I hugged her again and let her cry. After a minute or two she pulled away and dried her eyes with a tissue. "*Quien bien te quiere, te hará llorar*," she said. "Another of my mother's sayings. Who loves you well will make you cry."

We agreed that I'd stay at the condo and keep cleaning, while Lili took her mother's favorite dress over to the funeral home. "And combs for her hair," she said, as she rummaged through her mother's bureau.

"Do you think they put shoes on them? Should I take a pair of shoes, just in case?"

"I think you want her to go on to the next world the way she'd like."

"Then shoes. She had a pair of red high heels she always wore with this dress."

When she had everything packed in a hanging bag of her mother's, I stopped her for one more kiss before she left. *"Te amo mucho,"* I said. Then I smiled. "Did I get that right?"

"I'll make you into a Juban eventually." She smiled.

I was pleased to see that the recycling bin by the garbage chute had been emptied, so I filled it up with newspapers once more. Then I went into the kitchen and continued the cleanup there. I threw away a lot of rusted, bent or otherwise disfigured items.

Lili's mother had at least two or three of every kitchen accessory known to man, from pie wedges to slotted spoons, as well as a whole lot of items I could only guess at. I put together a box for Lili to review with the goal of donating to a charity. Once I had a shelf cleared, I scrubbed it clean, put out fresh shelf liner, and began organizing.

As I worked, I thought about Lili. She didn't seem to have pack rat tendencies—she'd become accustomed to traveling light in her photojournalism work, and when she'd moved in with me she'd brought little beyond her clothes, her photographs and her electronics.

Was her mother's behavior based on years of privation? On having to move so frequently? Or was it just a side effect of aging?

When she returned a few hours later, carrying bags from a local deli, she still looked very sad. "It was hard at the funeral home. Knowing it's the end. That I will never be the daughter she wanted me to be. 'A son is a son until he takes a wife, but a daughter is a daughter all her life.'"

I began unloading the bag of bagels, lox and cream cheese and other delicacies. "That's an English sentence that doesn't sound like one of your mother's Cuban proclamations."

"She'd never say it. Fedi was her little prince and she would never say a word against him, or by extension, Sara. They weren't even married yet when my mother started calling her Sarita and *mi chiquita*."

"And didn't she have nicknames for you?"

"Lili. Liliana when she was irritated. Liliana Estrella Weinstock when she was really angry." She crossed her arms over her chest. "Whereas Fedi was always *amado* or *azucar* or *mi perrito*." She stopped. "I can't think of Fedi's middle name. I never heard my mother call him all three names. Oh, wait. Federico David." She pronounced his middle name da-VEED.

She looked at me. "What did your parents call you?"

"My father called me noodnik," I said. "I thought it was a little love name, and it wasn't until I was a teenager that I realized it was Yiddish for pest."

She laughed.

"Of course I got my full name periodically. Steven Michael Levitan. My mother called me pussycat sometimes, and her mother called me Steve-e-leh. My uncle called me Stevarino. I was named after my father's father, who died just before I was born, and his Hebrew name was Shmuel Chaim. Sometimes my grandma called me that."

"It's funny how each person has so many names," Lili said. "Sometimes a name that's unique to one person, and when they die, no one will ever call you that again."

"If it makes you feel better, I can call you Liliana Estrella Weinstock sometimes."

She laughed. "We'll have to work on your accent. It's Es-tray-lyah." The rolling L was tough for me to manage, and we giggled together as I tried.

Chapter 7
Your Brother

The cemetery where Señora Weinstock was to lay beside her husband was a broad plain of headstones interspersed with the occasional tree or marble mausoleum. "Those people owned an electronics store in Miami," Lili said, pointing out one of the chapels as we drove toward the graveyard service. "My mother knew them from her shul. She used to say *"Como si su mierda no apestara?"*

Lili was peppering her speech with a lot more Spanish since our arrival in Miami. "*Mierda* means shit, right?" I asked.

"Like your shit doesn't stink," she said. "My mother was jealous that she couldn't build a mausoleum for my father."

"I think they're all in the same place, and all that matters is the people they leave behind, not the monuments."

"You're awfully wise these days." She pulled the rental car to a halt beside an open grave, with a green cloth awning over it. She squeezed my hand. "I am very glad you're here."

"Always an honor to be by your side, sweetheart."

As we got out of the car, she pinned a torn black ribbon to her blouse, the symbol of Jewish mourning. Fedi and Sara arrived behind us, with their two children, all of them dressed in black and wearing similar ribbons, which Lili said had been dispensed at the funeral home.

Fedi looked like an El Greco Jesus, thin and sad, with dark hair and a heart-shaped face like Lili's. He was surprisingly tall, a fact that Lili had never mentioned, at least six-four. Beside him, Sara looked like a gnome wife, with round cheeks and a black kerchief over her blonde hair.

Lili introduced us, and we touched cheeks and I told them both how sorry I was. Fedi's son was named Rafael, after his grandfather, Fedi added, and I realized I had never known Lili's father's name. Rafi was a skinny, gawky kid in his early teens, and his handshake was cool and clammy.

"And this is Isabella." Fedi brought forward a shy young girl of about ten. She was destined to be a beauty like her aunt, with Lili's auburn curls and that same heart-shaped face. "Bella Rebecca," Fedi continued. "She has my mother's Hebrew name, Bina, and Rivka, after Sara's mother. She's also named after my aunt Bella."

The rabbi pulled up and Lili and Fedi went to speak with him. "It's very sweet of you to come down here to support Lili," Sara said.

"We've been together three years," I said.

"Has it been that long? My, time flies. But then, Lili did not come to Florida very often to visit."

Interesting. I could see that Sara had as sharp a tongue as Lili's mother, and wondered if that was one of the reasons Fedi had been attracted to her.

Thank God my mother was a nice woman.

The rabbi's service was short, ending with, "People often call Miami God's Waiting Room, a place where the elderly come to spend their last years before they die. In Benita's case, she spent her years here engaging in her passions—swimming, collecting, and enjoying the love of her family."

Then Fedi spoke about his mother for a few minutes. As I expected, he had only good memories of her and the way she had called him *mi perrito*. "When we were finally able to get a puppy, I didn't know what to call him," Fedi said, and the crowd laughed.

I was surprised that Lili stood up to speak after Fedi. "My mother disagreed with many of the choices I made in my life," she said. "And that caused us to argue, probably more than we should have. But she was a fiery Latina, like me, and so perhaps it was inevitable. I hope she loved me as much as I loved her." She blew a kiss down to the coffin. "*Adios, mamita.*"

After a few more prayers, and the cemetery workers lowered the coffin into the ground, we took turns shoveling dirt onto the grave. Then the rabbi announced to the fifteen people assembled that we were all invited to join the family in sitting shiva at Fedi's home.

As Lili and I walked back to the rental car, her phone pinged with an incoming text, and she checked the message. "Condolences from Philip," she said, naming her first husband. "Always had impeccable timing."

"You told him your mother died?"

"Of course. She was his mother-in-law for a few years. Why wouldn't I tell him?"

"And Adriano, too?"

That was her first husband. "Adriano, too," she said. "Though his style is more to send a bouquet of flowers to our house. I'll bet it will arrive within a few hours after we get back to Stewart's Crossing. Adriano will check the mourning regulations and then flights back to Philadelphia, and time the arrival accordingly."

I shook my head. Lili had a full life before she met me, and there was no reason why she wouldn't continue to be in touch with people who had been close to her in the past.

But I was the one by her side at this sunbaked cemetery in Miami, and that was what mattered.

Lili clicked on Fedi's address in her phone, and we took off from the cemetery. As we reached the highway, my phone rang with Rick's tone.

"How's it going down there?" he asked.

"We just left the funeral. On our way to Lili's brother's house."

"Send her love from me and Tamsen."

"I will. How's Rochester?"

"I can walk each of them individually, and they behave beautifully, but when I walk them together they're like the devil on each other's shoulders. Pulling and jumping and making my life miserable. But dogs, you know?"

Rick was quiet for a moment, and I thought maybe the call had dropped. "This probably isn't a good time," he said. "Give me a call when you can talk."

I looked at Lili, and she nodded. "Lili's driving. I can talk."

"Remember that old man you found? Eckhardt Lalor?"

"I never knew his first name. What about him?"

"Did you know Jerry Faulkner at Pennsbury High?"

I was thrown for a second, but I focused. "Jerry. Faulkner. Big guy, kind of dumb? Played golf?"

"That's him. He runs a river rafting operation out of Potter's Harbor now. He does a regular cleanup of the riverbank on Monday afternoons, picking up junk his clients toss in the river. He stumbled on Lalor's body in the river on Monday."

"Oh, that's a shame."

"Yeah. I thought you'd want to know."

I thanked him, and Lili continued to navigate our way out to Fedi's house for shiva, and I remembered those I had lost. Friends, family, colleagues, neighbors. From the violent to the mundane. How much longer would Lili and I live side-by-side, with Rochester joining us? I reached over and squeezed her hand.

Chapter 8
Spic and Span

Fedi lived out in the Broward County suburbs in a rambling split-level house. There were already a couple of cars in the driveway and along the street. We spent a couple of hours there, talking to Lili's family, though since much of the conversation was in Spanish I spent most of my time either eating or helping clean up.

That evening, we were too tired to do much cleaning in the condo. But we spent all day Friday throwing away debris and organizing the items that Lili, Fedi and Sara wanted to keep. "Have you seen my mother's diamond engagement ring?" Lili asked, when we slouched on the sofa to take a break. "It's not in her jewelry box or in the safe."

I shook my head. "You think maybe she lost it?"

"I don't know, and that's what's frustrating. Maybe she took it off and put it down somewhere, and it got stuck under a pile. Or maybe it rolled under a piece of furniture and she couldn't get it."

We both stood up. "When my parents got married, they didn't have much money," Lili said. "My dad got my mom a gold band with a couple of tiny diamond chips in it, and he promised to buy her a better one when he could." She turned to look at me. "She never wanted one, but he bought her a big diamond for their twenty-fifth wedding anniversary."

"I'm sensing an undercurrent here. She didn't want one but he bought one anyway."

"Actually, that's not the point, though it is something to think about. She wore it while he was alive, because obviously it mattered to him, but when he died she put it away in her jewelry box and went back to her original ring."

We both got down on our knees and started looking, using one of the many flashlights that Benita had accumulated—though most of them had dead batteries. I took the bedroom and used a broom to sweep out the dust bunnies. No ring under the mechanized bed, or under the old-fashioned highboy and lowboy Benita used as dressers. I checked the bathroom, in the corners and behind the toilet. I took everything out of the vanity, filling a garbage can while I was at it, and came up empty.

I found Lili on the living room floor on her back. "Are you okay?"

She sat up. "Sure. I looked everywhere and I couldn't find it."

"Maybe Fedi has it. You want to call and ask him?"

"Not that big of an emergency. We'll see him and Sara tonight anyway."

We kept cleaning, right up until the time we had to leave to meet Fedi and Sara at Temple Beth Shmuel, the Cuban synagogue Lili's mother had belonged to. The exterior was an odd mix of misshapen concrete windows, but inside was like almost every synagogue I'd been to, a colorful ark on a bema surmounted by a *Ner Tamid*, the eternal light.

The service at Beth Shmuel reflected that mix of languages I had come to expect in Miami, blending English and Hebrew with a dollop of Spanish in the introduction and conversation. At least I knew when to stand and when to sit, and when to bow my head. We mourned Benita Weinstock and heard her name read out in the list of those observing shloshim, the first 30 days after a death.

We had a quick dinner with Fedi and Sara, and then returned to

Benita's apartment to keep cleaning. Saturday morning Lili and I swam in the ocean behind the condo, and then spent most of the day cleaning. I exchanged a couple of text messages with Rick: Rochester was fine, he and Rascal were having fun, he was eating his food and playing a lot.

Around four, Lili's phone rang. After a rapid conversation in Spanish, she hung up and said, "Fedi and Sara are on their way over to see how much we've done. We've got to get moving."

"Won't they be grateful we've done anything?" I asked, as Hurricane Lili began to sweep from room to room.

"We're leaving tomorrow, Steve," she said. "They're staying here. Everything I don't do will fall on Fedi's shoulders. I don't want him to complain about anything."

"Has he complained so far?"

"Of course he has," she said, tugging at a plastic bag that refused to leave the garbage can. "I was never here, remember? All the burden of taking care of my mother fell on him and Sara."

I took the bag from her and carried it out to the trash chute in the hallway, and when I returned Lili was scrubbing the kitchen counter. "Hey, hey," I said, taking her arm. "They know we've been staying here, right? They're not going to expect it to be spic and span."

Lili looked at me, and then began to laugh.

"What?"

"That phrase. The first time my mother heard it she thought it was derogatory about people who spoke Spanish. Spics."

"Did you explain it to her?"

"I was ten years old. I had no idea what it meant, only that Mrs. Goodwin across the hall in Kansas City said it about my mother's kitchen."

"It was a compliment."

"Cultural miscommunication. My mother never trusted Mrs. Goodwin after that."

I didn't know what to say. I'd heard someone use the phrase "Jew him down" in high school and been full of righteous indignation, until a friend pointed out I used "I got gypped" all the time, which was a slur against the Romany, or gypsy, people.

Box after box went down the trash chute, along with bent aluminum canes, broken dishes, and a large ceramic frog that Lili said was too ugly to donate to charity.

When Fedi and Sara arrived with Rafi and Bella, we trooped into the living room and Lili played hostess, making tiny cups of Cuban coffee and offering up some apple strudel she defrosted from one of her mother's many frozen containers.

"Sit, *hermana*," Fedi said eventually. "You don't have to wait on us."

Lili sat beside me on the sofa. The kids were on the floor by the sliding glass doors, playing on their phones, and Fedi and Sara sat on armchairs across from us.

"I'm impressed at how much cleaning you've done," Fedi said. "At least here in the living room. It doesn't look like a storage unit anymore."

The kids were hungry, but they didn't want to eat any of the food their grandmother had frozen, so we ordered a couple of pizzas. While we waited for the delivery, Lili and I cleared the dining room table, and Fedi and Sara walked through the apartment. They were full of compliments about the work we'd done, though it always seemed like we hadn't done enough

"What are we going to do about all the photo albums?" Fedi asked when we were eating.

"I can digitize the photos and send them to you," Lili said. "Neither of us really want those dusty old albums, right?"

"Just the photos," Fedi said. He turned to me. "Has Lili told you how many places we lived after we left Cuba?"

"Mexico and Kansas City?" I asked.

"And after Kansas City we moved to Nevada for a year. There's a picture somewhere of us at the Hoover Dam. My father was an engineer, you know, and he was always on the lookout for a better job, more money, more security. From Nevada we went to Illinois for two years—what was that city, *mamita?*" He looked at Lili.

"Buffalo Grove. Though we called it Buffalo Grave."

Fedi laughed. "I remember I had trouble with the word buffalo. I used to say it boof-a-low."

"From there we went to Long Island, and we had to learn to be Jewish American Princes and Princesses," Lili said. "I didn't fit in very well there, as you can imagine. I was glad to escape for college."

We had a good dinner, and I was pleased to get to know Fedi and Sara better. I imagined that we would spend some holidays together, perhaps Christmas in Florida every year, and that eventually I would think of them as the siblings I wished I had growing up.

Well, we'd done what we could. If we had to, we could fly down again for another few days to help out. But for now, I was eager to get home, back to my townhouse and my dog.

Chapter 9
Getting Muddy

We returned Lili's rental car at Miami airport early Sunday morning and we were on the ground in Philadelphia by noon. After we retrieved my car from the long-term lot I drove to River Bend and dropped Lili and our luggage off. She said she'd start a load of laundry, and I rode over to Tamsen and Rick's house. From the front yard I heard stereo barking, and I could easily distinguish Rochester's low barks from Rascal's higher-pitched yips.

I rang the bell, and as soon as Tamsen opened it for me the dogs tackled me. "Looks like someone is glad to see you," Tamsen said. "How's Lili holding up?"

"She's very sad, but coming to terms with it. The heart attacks her mother had in the hospital really surprised everyone, and it's taken her a while to let it all sink in."

"I'll call her tonight," Tamsen said.

I was finally able to sit on the floor and let the dogs jump over me. Rochester licked my right ear and I laughed. "Yes, I missed you, too, puppy."

Rick came downstairs and laughed as Rochester and I enjoyed our family reunion.

"Can I talk to you for a minute?" he asked.

"Sure." I left the dogs to their play and followed him into Tamsen's office, which was lined with samples of the promotional items she brokered. Engravable photo frames, a towel shaped like a surfboard, an explosion of pens and sticky notes.

Rick leaned up against Tamsen's desk and motioned me to her ergonomic leather chair. "That guy you met by the river? Mr. Lalor?"

"Yeah, you told me someone discovered his body in the river. You think he went wandering and fell in?"

"That's what his family would like me to believe. But I'm not so sure."

"Did he drown?"

"That's what the medical examiner says. Water in the lungs, which means he was still breathing when he went in."

I leaned forward. "But you disagree?"

"The ME's cause of death is drowning, and the verdict is death by misadventure." He paused again for what seemed like a long time. "I went up to Potter's Harbor to talk to Jerry yesterday. He said that up by his operation, the river runs consistently south, but around Trenton the flow is affected by the tides coming up from Delaware Bay. If Lalor went into the river around the layby across from Crossing Estates, his body should have been carried due south. But instead he was found about a mile north of there."

Rick started walking toward the window, which looked out onto the back yard. I could see that tree where Rochester had found Tamsen's gold necklace. Instead he stopped at Tamsen's desk and turned on her computer. "Let me show you on the map."

I was jealous; Tamsen's computer was a lot faster than mine, and quickly Rick had brought up Google Maps. "See this island in the river, here?"

He pointed to a long, vaguely oval shape. Then he pointed farther south, just past the end of the island, to Crossing Estates and the layby east of it. "That's where we've been assuming that Lalor went in the water, because that's the closest access point to his son's house."

He indicated the top of the island. The channel between the mainland and the island narrowed to a choke point a few hundred feet sound of the end. "This is where Jerry found Lalor's body. According to him, there's no way the river could have washed him that far north."

"How wide is the channel there?" I asked.

"Maximum six feet, and only about two feet deep. Jerry says that when people drop stuff out of their rafts as they're floating downriver, it often accumulates there. He goes down there every week in summer to clean it out."

Rick turned away from the computer and leaned back against the windowsill.

"You think he went into the river farther north of that choke point," I said. "But that's too far for him to walk. Which means someone had to drive him up there."

Rick nodded.

"And that someone might have pushed him into the river, instead of him slipping in on his own."

"That's it in a nutshell. But I can't legitimately investigate, because there's no crime involved."

"Even with this evidence from Jerry?"

Rick frowned. "Jerry's a good guy, but he's not the most reliable witness. Last Monday, by his own account, he'd had a couple of beers while he was pulling trash out of the river. He said he found Lalor north of the choke point, but then he admitted to me yesterday that maybe his sense of direction was a bit impaired."

"So you want me to look into Lalor's death." It wasn't a question, merely a statement.

"Do you think you could? Work some of your magic?"

I blew out a small breath. "I can try."

Rick paused again for a long moment. "Thanks."

Rochester and I had helped Rick with a number of his cases in the past, because both the dog and I were nosy, and because I knew and cared about the victims. Gradually Rick had come to accept the way that Rochester was often able to indicate clues to us, and part of our friendship had been built on working together to solve some complicated puzzles.

I had occasionally been able to use my computer search skills—almost always legitimately—to help him find information, too.

But this was the first time he had directly asked for my help. It meant something, but I wasn't sure what. That he trusted me, believed in Rochester? I understood that. But he'd always been confident that with or without my help, he'd solve the mystery and bring the criminal to justice.

Now, the chief and the ME had tied his hands, and I was the only one he trusted enough to voice his fears and ask for help. I had heard someone on a podcast say recently that it was great to be the person people asked for help—being able to provide advice and favors and even manual labor for a friend was a boost to one's ego. But he warned that those who never asked for help risked losing those very relationships. No one wants to seem the weaker partner in a friendship, the one who always needs help and never has the opportunity to provide it.

I'd been asking for Rick's help for years, for everything from police information to dog-sitting, and it felt good to be able to do something for him in return.

"I should probably let you get back. I'll get you Rochester's stuff."

We walked to the kitchen together, where Rochester and Rascal were sprawled on the tile, back to back. As soon as Rochester heard the rattle of his leash he jumped up, and he and Rascal kept getting underfoot as Rick helped me carry the food, bowls and toys to the car. Back inside, I hooked Rochester's leash and said goodbye to Rascal, Tamsen and Rick. There was still a bit of a tumult as I struggled to get Rochester out the front door without Rascal following. Rick had to grab hold of the Aussie's collar to keep him back.

My last look as I closed the door was Rascal's sad eyes staring at me. I was taking away his best friend.

Rochester kept sniffing me on the way home, as if he wasn't sure I

Dog's Waiting Room

was really there. "Come on, dog," I said eventually. "I left you for less than a week. And you had fun with Rascal while I was gone."

He rested his head on my right thigh, drooling onto my leg, but I didn't mind. I had missed him, and I was glad to be back with him.

He was excited to see Lili, too, taking off as soon as I opened the door to gallop through the house in search of her. Then I put out all his favorite toys and played with him on the living room floor.

I had forgotten to shut off the delivery of the local paper, the Bucks County Courier Times, while we were away, so I had a stack of them on the coffee table to glance through before chucking them into the recycle bin.

Lili called me upstairs to help find her phone charger, and when I returned to the living room Rochester had knocked the papers from their neat pile into a mess on the floor. He had started to tear up the B section of one of the papers when I got there and snatched it from his claws.

I was surprised to see an article on the front page, below the fold, headlined "Developer Dies in Delaware Drowning."

It had been published the day after Eckhardt Lalor's death, before the medical examiner had provided his final ruling. The author quoted several neighbors who said that Lalor often was caught wandering around the neighborhood, and the reporter noted that there was no barrier along the Delaware in the area where Lalor went into the water.

"Good boy," I said, scratching behind Rochester's ears as I read. "You know we're on Mr. Lalor's case, don't you?"

He yawned and showed me his full rows of teeth, and his long pink tongue curled out like a magic carpet. I smiled at him. "How'd you like to go for a ride?"

He jumped up and began dancing around me. I called upstairs, "Lili, I'm going to take Rochester out for a while. You'll be OK?"

"I'm going to start digitizing photos while the laundry runs," she answered. "Have fun."

Then the doorbell rang. Lili looked at her watch. "Right on time."

"You're expecting someone?"

"I told you. Adriano will send flowers for my mother."

She opened the door, and sure enough, a young man stood there with a huge floral arrangement in his arms. She thanked the boy and took the flowers. "Don't ask me how he does it. It's just a weird talent of his."

On my way out of the house, I called Rick. "You have a few minutes? I'm taking Rochester along the river to see if we can find where he went in."

"The crime scene team haven't been able to find it," Rick said. "But then, they were looking only within walking distance of Jeffrey Lalor's house. Jerry Faulkner said there's a layby a few hundred yards south of a street called Spring Court. I'll meet you there. Maybe the death dog will come up with something."

I hated to hear Rochester called the death dog. I preferred clue-finding canine or doggy detective, but I had to give Rick his due. There had been dead bodies involved in our investigations in the past.

As I drove along River Road, I pulled up a map on my phone. It looked like Spring Court was a big U-shape with both a north and south connection to River Road. I'd have to cruise along until I found the layby.

Fortunately Rick got there first, so I was able to pull in behind his truck. The island was between us and the main body of the river, so all I could see were the willows along the mainland, and a copse of tree across a shallow, weed-splattered channel.

"No chance to get any tire impressions here," Rick said. "Too much time has passed, and Jerry's big truck probably wiped out anything that was here before it." He nodded forward. "Jerry said the choke point is a bit to the north of us here." He led the way down a narrow path that wove around maples and oaks that had been there when Washington prowled this area, looking for a way across to Trenton.

Rochester and I followed him, stopping at the same place, where a couple of thin shoots of a maple tree had been trampled. I leaned down and pointed to a single long thread in a bright scarlet color. "Any idea what Lalor was wearing the day he died?"

"Rutgers T-shirt that was way too loose on him and a pair of jeans," Rick said. "Sneakers with almost no tread left on his feet."

"Got an evidence bag? That thread is close to the Rutgers scarlet."

"How would you know that?"

"I went to Eastern, remember? We played Rutgers in football. There's a big placard in the gym with all the mascots from the opposing teams. Rutgers is the Scarlet Knight."

Rick just shook his head and bagged the thread.

I looked around, and through the narrow screen of trees to the west side of us. There wasn't steady traffic on Route 32, but what there was moved quickly and there was no sidewalk.

"How did Lalor usually get to the river?" I asked.

"The layby where you park? There's a corn field there, with a hedgerow."

"Like at Honey Hollow?" That was an environmental education center we'd been bussed to back in middle school, where we learned that a hedgerow was a line of wild shrubs that held refuge for small animals, bees and other insects.

"Exactly. There's a dirt path between the hedgerow and the field that leads directly to the line of trees that border Crossing Estates."

I nodded. "When the ME examined him, was he dehydrated?"

Rick pursed his lips. "Not particularly."

"When Rochester and I met him he was. And he'd only been out of the house for an hour or two. If he'd walked all the way from Stewart's Crossing here he'd be in bad shape."

"Which means someone had to drive him," Rick said.

Rochester wanted to sniff something closer to the channel, so we started in that direction, the dog leading us on a scuffed path. "Hold up," Rick said. He moved around us and got down on one knee.

"More bent tree shoots," he said. "And the dead leaf cover on the ground has been disturbed, too."

He stood up. "It could mean something, or it could just be Jerry Faulkner dragging a trash can. We'd need to find a big honking clue if I'm going to get the chief to open up this case again."

"Let Rochester have a go," I said. I eased up on his leash and he moved forward, lifting each paw delicately because he must have sensed there were thorns around. He sniffed a lot, nose down, and at one point I laughed and said, "Rochester, you're acting like a scent-hound. Do you have some beagle or foxhound in you?"

"I think the best dogs surprise you with their ability to do stuff they aren't bred for," Rick said. "Rascal's a herding dog, but he can fetch with the best of them."

"Rochester has never understood the point of fetching," I said. "If I throw a ball to him, he runs and grabs it and then starts chewing."

We watched as Rochester moved forward, veering closer to the riverbank, where the trees thinned out and the slippery leaves and mud made the undergrowth more dangerous. "Slowly, puppy," I said, holding tight to his leash.

He stopped suddenly, about a foot from the river's edge. I looked back, and though we'd only come about thirty or forty feet, the layby was completely invisible—which meant no one could see us from the street.

Rick got down to the ground again. "Look at this mud," he said, pointing with a stick. "That look like a slide to you?"

I kept hold of Rochester and knelt down beside Rick. "Yup. You can see two heelprints there, and then a long trench right up to the water."

I stood up. "What do we do now?"

"You wait here. I have some footprint cast material back at my truck. It's not enough to move forward on yet, but at some point, if I have more evidence, I can reopen the case and match the footprints to Lalor's shoes."

While we waited for Rick to return, I told Rochester what a good boy he was. But with my head so close to his, I could smell that he needed a bath soon—especially once I realized that his golden paws and lower legs were splattered with dark mud.

Rick returned and took some photos and casts of the footprints in the mud. "So what do you think?" I asked. "Is this murder? Or still death by misadventure?"

"You know, because we've gone over this a bunch of times. For a murder, you need means, motive and opportunity. Right now the closest I can come is means—but even if someone was with him, he could have slipped down that slope himself."

"Which means I need to see who had a motive to get Mr. Lalor out of the way." I felt that old familiar tingling in my fingertips, a sudden desire to get my laptop and start snooping around places I wasn't supposed to be.

"Legitimately," Rick said, as if he was reading my mind. "If it looks like we need bank records or anything protected, that's on me to request."

I wanted to argue. How could he know what to ask for if I didn't dig around first? But instead the angel on my other shoulder said, "I understand that. But there's still a lot of digging I can do legitimately. Lalor told me he used to own a lot of property. Those records are all public. I can dig around and see if there's anything unusual in those transactions. I can check social media, see if any of his kids or grandkids look like they're living above their means."

"I know you can do all that. And I appreciate anything you can find."

We shook hands, and then Rochester and I went back to my car, where I put a towel over the passenger seat and let Rochester in. (A smart golden daddy always keeps a couple of clean towels in reserve.)

When we got home, I marched him right up to the Roman tub in the master bathroom, and while Lili held him on the tile floor I ran the tub, stripped and climbed in.

Bathing an eighty-pound golden like Rochester is a two-human operation. Lili lifted his front paws over the rim of the tub once I had the water at the right temperature, and I tugged forward as Lili lifted his hindquarters.

"Our next dog is going to be a smaller model," she said, when she stood up. Rochester looked balefully at her, his feet in the water up to his elbows and knees. I had learned early on to call the first joint on his front legs his elbows, and the joint on the back legs his knees. It avoided a lot of confusion when reporting something to the vet.

Then I rinsed him with a plastic pitcher, soaped him up with special shampoo for special dogs (well, it was actually coal tar and sulfur with aloe but I wanted him to feel special.) Lots of rinsing and wringing out his coat followed, until he was ready for Lili to come over with a big pile of towels.

She got the first towel up in front of her like a shield before he shook, spraying water back on me instead. "Thank you, my darling boy," I said. I leaned over the tub and dried his back end, while Lili took care of his front end and his undercarriage. As soon as he could, he scampered away from us, shook vigorously, then jumped on the bed to dry himself further on the comforter.

"I was going to wash that tomorrow anyway," Lili said. She left me a clean towel and took the pile of wet ones downstairs to the laundry.

I emptied the tub of muddy brown water and refilled it, then took a bath myself. By the time I joined Rochester on the bed we were both lean, clean machines.

Well, I wasn't as lean as I could be, but he was still in fighting shape. "You did a good job today, puppy," I said. "Finding the place where Mr. Lalor went into the water. I'm sorry we weren't there to rescue him a second time."

He looked up at me sadly, then nestled his wet head against the towel around my waist and rubbed.

Chapter 10
Miss Melantha

I didn't have anything pressing waiting for me at Friar Lake on Monday morning, so I decided to extend my vacation an extra day. After breakfast I helped Lili put away all the clean clothes and freshly-washed towels, and then she left for a half-day at her office.

For a moment I stood in the living room and stared at the arrangement her ex had sent. White roses, white lilies, and miniature white carnations, artfully arranged with some green and purple vegetation, in an elegant dark blue vase. Classy and somber, yet not overly funereal.

On rare occasions I found myself in competition with Lili's ex-husbands. They lived glamorous lifestyles, they had money, they had taste. But then again I had Lili.

I had suggested to Rick that I could survey the records of property Eckhardt Lalor had owned, or might still own, and see if there was anything unusual in the transactions. So I opened my laptop to do that, with Rochester curled around the back of my chair, chewing on one of his plastic rubber bones.

When he was a puppy, I gave him adorable stuffed toys to play with. He destroyed them within minutes, biting off the ears of a dachshund decorated as a hot dog, chewing through the neck of a giraffe, spreading lambswool all over the floor.

Then I moved on to plastic toys. A Christmas elf was quickly eviscerated. A long-necked chicken that squawked when squeezed suffered a thoracotomy via Rochester's jaws.

The simplest solutions ended up the best. Hard rubber bones, some with bumps for extra jaw interest. Strong ropes with knots at each end for tugging. Lili and I called the bone he was currently chewing the "penis bone" because he'd already chewed off the blobs on one end, leaving him with a very phallic-shaped remainder.

Rochester chewed behind me as I began with Lalor's obituary, which popped up easily. "Eckhardt Lalor, STEWART'S CROSSING. Eckhardt Lalor passed away June 4, 2014. He was a sixth-generation Trentonian and a graduate of Trenton High and Rutgers University. He served in the Army during the Korean War, and returned home to begin a long career in property management. Son of the late Hamilton Lalor and Virginia Nottingham Lalor, he was married to Marie Innocenza for ten years, and is survived by their children Jeffrey (Vivian), Anita (Frank Quinton) and Peter. Then he was married to the late Jane (Turpin) Nitz and is survived by their children Clifford (Rebecca) and Elaine, as well as Jane's children Robert and Susan. His third marriage ended in divorce. He is survived by many loving grandchildren."

Man, that was a lot of names. I was glad the obituary hadn't mentioned all the names of his grandchildren. I did remember his crack about the initials of his kids—Jeffrey, Anita and Peter, and the way he'd called them little JAPs.

The obit included the funeral services, which were to be held the following afternoon at Ewing Cemetery, on the north side of the city.

After the obit, I continued searching online for mentions of Lalor's name. I quickly discovered that if there was a bad neighborhood in Trenton, Lalor owned property there. I found numerous articles in the old *Trentonian* morning paper, and the Trenton *Times*, about substandard living conditions at his apartment buildings.

Tenants complained that they had no heat in the winter, that their roofs leaked and their kitchens were infested with roaches. Several times he had been cited by housing inspectors, and once a man named Solomon Jackson had organized a rent strike among Lalor's tenants.

Through it all Lalor was non-committal. He explained that the roofs were old and prone to leaks, and that he responded to complaints. He blamed the roaches on poor sanitary habits of his tenants. He had been fined numerous times, and as he got into his seventies, he began selling off properties.

Because he used a variety of different corporate names for property records it was hard to tell what he still owned, but I decided that I'd put off further searching in lieu of a look around. I hadn't been to the areas of Trenton where Lalor owned his properties since I was a kid, and I wanted to scope out the lay of the land.

Rochester accompanied me as I drove to the Scudder Falls Bridge and over the river there, then down Route 29 toward the city. It was a trip down memory lane for me—we'd often gone that way when my father or mother was dropping me off at Sunday school or Hebrew school. I still remembered once, long before, when we'd been driving along and my mother had spotted her uncle, in his signature maroon Buick. "There's Uncle Lou," she had said. "Wave hello!"

She beeped and we waved, and Uncle Lou waved back, and it was one of those moments when I realized that the world wasn't all about me. Usually when we saw Uncle Lou it was because we went to his house, or he came to ours. I suddenly understood that everyone else had lives, separate from their intersections with me.

It was a realization that came back to me in force as I approached the Parkside Avenue exit, where I still remembered seeing Uncle Lou in his Buick. On an impulse, I took that exit and drove alongside Cadwalader Park.

The monkey house, Lalor had said, when we'd talked. He could always tell when his kids had been there, because they smelled. I pulled into a parking spot on Parkside Avenue and looked up on my phone where the Lalor house had been. Then I drove into the park on Hillvista Boulevard and did a circle around Ellarslie Mansion, long since refurbished and the monkey house destroyed.

It was an impressive Italian-style villa, centered in the last urban park designed by Frederic Law Olmstead, who put together New York's Central Park. It was a fact of much pride to my mother, who loved the city of her birth and was proud of many random features, like the shaky bridge along the Delaware designed by John Roebling, who also constructed the Brooklyn Bridge. In addition to being the capital of New Jersey, Trenton had once been an important industrial city, and my mother had treasured those monuments.

I exited the park onto Stuyvesant Avenue, and a turn onto Beechwood found me in front of the big Queen Anne style house where Eckhardt Lalor had raised his family. The ground floor and sprawling porch had been converted into a daycare center, and a tumble of black and brown kids played there with giant plastic blocks in a rainbow of colors. A small sliding board at one corner was very popular.

The upper floors appeared to be residential, from the clothes on a line and the sheets tacked up over windows. An older Black woman was working in the yard, picking up kids' toys, and she asked, "Can I help you?"

"Just looking around," I said. "Do you know, did Lalor Properties own this house?"

"Mister Lalor himself, and his family," the woman said. "I should know. I cleaned house for them the last ten years or so."

Rochester settled by my feet, chewing a tree branch.

"You know he died?" I asked the woman.

She nodded. "Not soon enough. He was not a good man." She peered at me. "You know him?"

I held out my hand. "My name's Steve, and this is Rochester. We found Mr. Lalor walking along the river a couple of weeks ago and helped him get home." I held my hand out to her, and she shook it.

The outside of her hand was leathery, but the palm was a smooth peach color, lined with deep veins.

"My name's Melantha. This here's my daughter's day care."

"Looks very well kept. Sorry to bother you. I just felt bad about his dying, and I was curious what kind of a person he was. Was he a bad boss?"

"I don't care what no white man says to me. I put up with a load of bad in my life, and I still got more to live, God willing. But he was mean to those children."

"Did he hit them?"

Melantha shook her head. "No, he was too smart for that. I came to help when the first Mrs. Lalor was sick. He never once went to the doctor with her, that I know. And he wanted her to have all three kids fed and in their rooms by the time he got home." She shook her head. "Sick as she was."

A boy and a girl came up to the gate, and Rochester stepped forward so they could touch him. "He be all right?" Melantha asked.

"Absolutely. He's a sweetheart."

She unlocked the wire gate and we stepped inside, and immediately Rochester began to play with the two kids, and then others rushed over. Soon he was on his back, waving his legs in the air, and the kids were petting and scratching him.

While Rochester played I thought back to Eckhardt Lalor. He had seemed like such a sweet old man when I met him, but I was seeing a different side of him through this woman and through my search of the properties he'd owned.

Melantha invited me to sit on a stone bench under the oak tree. "What happened when the first Mrs. Lalor died?" I prompted.

"He had a sister come live with them then, to take care of the children, and she was just as mean as he was. I didn't come back to cleaning again until he married Miz Jane." She smiled. "Now there was a sweet woman. Schoolteacher, two kids of her own, just scratching by. Living in one of his buildings, and she complained about the hot water."

Melantha grinned broadly, showing a missing lower tooth. "She went right up to his office to speak to him, and what do you know, three months later she was married and looking after five children. That's when I come back to help."

Rochester looked up from playing with the kids, as if he was curious.

"Did she change him? Miz Jane?"

"Not one bit, though she tried mightily. I'd hear her lecturing him, one or twice after dinner, about paying more attention to those children. But he didn't want nothing of it."

She leaned back against the oak tree, a couple of brightly colored balls in her hands. "Then after her second baby was born, she was awful sick. I don't think she ever recovered from it."

"That's very sad."

One of the little girls came over to us. "Can we have a ball for the dog, Granny Mel?"

"I'll warn you, he doesn't fetch very well," I said, but she handed the girl the two balls she had in her hands. The girl rushed back to her friends, and then she threw the ball down the yard.

Rochester jumped up and raced after it. I thought I knew what to expect. He'd sit down and start chewing it. But he surprised me. He ran back, dropped the ball in front of the girl, and sat on his haunches, his mouth wide open in a doggy grin.

I had never seen him play fetch like that before and I watched as he fetched once more. It was only when Melantha started talking again that I turned my attention back to her.

"It was terrible. Specially hard on her two, Bobby and Susie. They were orphans, you see, and in mortal fear that he'd turn them over to an agency." She straightened her shoulders and stood up. "That's when he hired Miss Jenny. I was right there, could have taken care of the whole lot of them, but he said he couldn't have a colored woman living in his house."

She frowned. "I washed my hands of them. Felt terrible about leaving those kids, but I wasn't coming back where I wasn't wanted."

"How'd you end up back here, then?"

"My daughter, Renee. She was in the Army, you see, and she saved up some money. She had just come out and wanted to start a business, and when I saw this house was for sale I told her that despite everything, Mr. Lalor had always kept his own house up nice. And then Mr. Jeffrey learned that I was Renee's mother, and he said he appreciated all I had done for his family, and he gave Renee a good price."

"I'm glad."

A middle-aged woman, her skin a few shades lighter than Melantha's, opened the front door then. "Mama? Can you come in and give me a hand?"

"I got to go," Melantha said. "I don't like to wish ill of the dead, but if there is a God, then I hope Mr. Lalor is hot and sweating mightily."

I thanked her and wished her and Renee well with the day care. The kids trailed in behind Melantha, and I opened the gate so that Rochester and I could leave.

"Did you have fun, puppy?" I asked, as we walked down the block. "Maybe I need to find you some little kids to play with."

He simply grinned and panted.

Most of the other houses on the street, once miniature mansions, had been left to the vagaries of man and nature. Broken windows, beer bottles in yards, a rustled bicycle in parts, the scraggly remains of what had once been beautiful rose gardens.

A couple looked like they had been lovingly maintained, despite the fall of the neighborhood around them. One house had a fresh coat of paint, another a front porch so new I could see the green grain of the wood.

We went back to the car and cruised around the neighborhood. Had Eckhardt Lalor contributed to the downfall of this area? I pulled up addresses of properties he had owned and drove slowly through the decaying parts of the city of my birth.

Rochester, usually so eager to stick his head out the window and experience the world around him, remained on the passenger seat, his head on my lap. It hurt my heart to see the conditions so many people lived in. Was that the fault of landlords like Lalor? Or, as he'd been quoted saying, because the tenants didn't keep the places up?

We ended up in a sad part of the city near the Battle Monument, a square platform with a fluted column mounted on it. On the very top, a statue of George Washington surveyed the area, a reminder of the Battle of Trenton which had been so important in the Revolutionary War.

I remembered how vibrant the area had been, and all the hours I'd spent in the Trenton Public Library nearby. I spotted a small pocket park named after Solomon Jackson, and pulled over in front of it. Why was that name familiar? Was he one of those many heroes of the Revolutionary War I had learned about as a kid?

Rochester was eager to get out of the car and sniff and pee, and I walked over to look at the plaque at the entrance to the park.

"Solomon Jackson was a Trenton native and community organizer who founded Take Back Trenton, a nonprofit organization that fought for tenant rights throughout the city. This park honors his life and work."

I looked around and didn't feel threatened, so I sat on a bench, pulled out my phone, and did some research on Mr. Jackson. I learned that he grew up in the slums off State Street, the rattle of the railroad the soundtrack to his life. He was seventeen during the 1967 riots, and he had been arrested for vandalism and sent to what was then called Trenton State Prison.

According to an online biography, he had been radicalized in prison, where he quickly got his GED, returned to his Baptist roots, and completed most of the requirements for an associate's degree. As soon as he was released, he became a community organizer and continued in college, eventually gaining a master's degree from Rutgers.

I stood up and went back to the plaque, which showed a stately

Black man with short dreadlocks. "Mr. Solomon, he did his part," a man said from beside me.

I looked over and saw an elderly Black man, skinny as a doctor's office skeleton, standing beside me. "Did you know him?" I asked.

"Sho thing. Back maybe twenty years ago, one a them hurricanes came through, flooded the streets and knocked out our power. When the power company take too long to get it back, because you know Black folk less important than white folk, Mr. Solomon gets a bunch a people to protest. Then the power came back, yes it did."

He nodded emphatically. "When the roofs start to leak, he find out who owns the buildings and go after them. That's the thing with folks on the welfare, we got time on our hands to go protest. Many the time I stood beside him, waving my signs."

"Sounds like a good man."

"He were indeed. Now his son done took up his mantle, the one from the AME Zion church. He ain't no Mr. Solomon, but he do try."

With a final pet on Rochester's head, the old man wandered away, and we went back to my car. By the time Rochester and I left the city to return home, it was clear that Lalor and men like him had done terrible things to the people and the landscape of Trenton. Was that enough of a motivation to kill him, though?

From the car, I called Rick. "I did some research on Eckhardt Lalor," I said. "You know he was a slumlord in Trenton?"

"I didn't. But his son lives in a mini-mansion in Crossing Estates, so that money has to come from somewhere. The son says he's 'between opportunities' right now, which means unemployed to me. That's one of the reasons I find the old man's death suspicious."

"I saw online that the funeral is tomorrow afternoon. As long as nothing urgent has come up at Friar Lake, I'll be able to leave there early and make to the cemetery."

"You're going to his funeral? But you didn't even know him."

"I met him, the once," I said. "I figure that's enough connection to start talking to people. And you asked me to snoop, remember."

"All right. Just be careful."

"Rick. No one is going to knife me or shoot me at the funeral just because I ask a couple of questions."

"I never know with you."

Chapter 11
Family Reunion

I wanted to spend some time Monday night researching Mr. Lalor and his family, but Lili had begun digitizing some of her mother's photo albums, and she wanted to share some of what she found with me.

There were black and white snapshots of her mother as a child, along with some of the cousins I'd met at the funeral. Then stunning photos of Benita as a young woman, posed on the beach like a bathing beauty. "She was beautiful, wasn't she?" Lili asked.

"I don't know." I reached over and used my index finger to turn Lili's face into profile. "She's OK. You have her best features, but something more."

"Steve."

"It's true. She's pretty, but she already looks like she's been beaten down by fate. What was going on in her life then?"

Lili pursed her lips. "I'd say she's in her early twenties in this picture. Her father passed away when she was nineteen, and mother worked at a guayabera factory. She specialized in embroidering the vertical stripes. People used to say they could always recognize one of her shirts because the embroidery was so beautiful."

She flipped another page to a group of young people out at a bar.

Benita was smiling there, next to a handsome man with a mustache and a porkpie hat. "Is that your father?"

"No. Probably just some guy at the bar."

I cocked my head. "Look at the way she's looking at him. I recognize that look."

"You only met my mother once, and you're an expert on her facial expressions."

"No, sweetheart, I'm an expert on yours. You look at me like that sometimes."

A slight flush rose in Lili's cheeks and she pulled the picture out of the album and turned it over. On the back was written "*A la Floridita con Juan Diego.*"

"Oh," Lili said.

"What's oh?"

"Juan Diego. My mother said he was an old beau of hers when she was young. His family owned all the Sinclair gas stations on the island. Remember, the ones with the dinosaur logo?"

"What happened?"

"He wasn't Jewish, and her mother didn't approve. And he had gone to college in the US, so his parents didn't want him to marry the uneducated daughter of a seamstress."

"What was Benita doing?"

"She was a secretary in the engineering department at the *Universidad de La Habana*. That's where she met my father, when he was a student there."

She flipped through a couple of photographs and found one with Señor Weinstock. "There. That's one from when they were dating. You're right, she's not looking at him the way she looked at Juan Diego."

"Was it a love match, do you think, or more a marriage of convenience?"

"I think he loved her more than she loved him," Lili said after a while. "Not that she didn't love him, or appreciate what he did for us. Often, when he got a new job, he would go on ahead of us, find a house for us, and then notify my mother to bring us. And he traveled a lot for his job."

We looked through more pictures, and though I meant to talk to her about Eckhardt Lalor the time wasn't right.

The next morning I dressed in a pair of black slacks with a white short-sleeved shirt. I figured that was good enough for the service for a man I hardly knew. And it was my second funeral in two weeks, and Lili had already taken my dark suit to the cleaners.

I would have an accumulation of chores to accomplish at Friar Lake, emails to answer and so on. But I still wanted to do some searching on Mr. Lalor before I went to the funeral, so I took my second laptop with me. It was an older model and had once belonged to Caroline Kelly, Rochester's original mom. When she died, I snuck it out of her house and put all my computer hacking tools on it.

I had just returned to Stewart's Crossing after a year in California's penal system for hacking, so that was a big deal. If my parole officer had found me in possession of those tools, he could have sent me right back to prison. But I needed to know who killed Caroline, so I took the risk.

Since then, I had struggled with my addiction to hacking. I belonged to an online support group, and I told Rick and Lili every time I used the laptop. Most of the time it had been to help Rick with his investigations, and of course to satisfy my own curiosity.

It took me a couple of hours to deal with all the emails and meeting requests and phone messages. One email was from Ewan Garrett, an assistant professor of philosophy at Eastern with whom I'd served on a committee in the past. He wanted to know if Friar Lake could be rented to non-profit organizations, and if it was available that Saturday.

I was embarrassed that I had taken nearly a week to answer him because I'd been in Florida, so I called him and apologized. "I'm sorry, I was out of town last week for a funeral," I said.

"Then you missed the huge thunderstorm on Wednesday," Ewan

said. "My son was absolutely terrified. But don't worry about getting back to me. I should have contacted you with more notice."

"What's up?"

"I belong to the local chapter of a national group, Parents without Partners, and we had a picnic scheduled for this Saturday. Unfortunately, the park we were going to use had some bad wind damage to its pavilions during that storm, and they had to shut down on an emergency basis."

"That's why you were asking about Friar Lake," I said. "I have nothing on the books Saturday. Did you still want to come over?"

"That would be a lifesaver," Evan said. "So many of our moms and dads are divorced, and they have to make plans far in advance to take the kids out. We had a plan for eleven o'clock. Does that work for you?"

"Sure." I went over the terms with him; because he was affiliated with Eastern, and represented a non-profit group, there would no charge for the use of the facility, though if they left a mess behind there might be a cleanup fee.

"Don't worry, a couple of our moms are very environmentally conscious. Leave no trace behind. We'll be good."

I said I'd email him the paperwork, and then Rochester and I walked out to Joey's office to let him know about the picnic. One of us had to be on-site if we had after-hours events, and we usually split the duties, but since I'd been away for the past week I planned to take it on. Plus I liked Ewan, and I was surprised that a guy so young was a single parent.

As we walked and Rochester sniffed, I realized Ewan wasn't that young. If he'd gone straight to graduate school from college, and completed his dissertation on the shortest schedule, he was close to thirty. My dad had been married, and I'd been born, before that milestone.

Was Ewan divorced? Widowed? Had he assumed custody of someone else's child, or had he decided to become a dad on his own?

Dog's Waiting Room

I reminded myself it was none of my business. I had the Lalor family to snoop into, and no reason to add Ewan to my list.

Joey was happy to let me take on the Saturday shift; he'd promised to drive his partner Mark to a big flea market in search of stock for Mark's antique business. Joey and I spent about an hour together going over what had happened on the property that I ought to know about.

"The storm passed us by," he said. "Landed south of here, down by Levittown. Did some damage to houses and stores down there, then swept up the center of the county, staying west of us."

"Good. Rick didn't mention anything about a storm when we talked, so I knew it didn't hit Stewart's Crossing."

We talked so long that I didn't get a chance to use any hacker tools. All I could do before I left Friar Lake was use my regular computer and a combination of Facebook and Google to identify the major family members I expected to see that afternoon.

Then I had to run Rochester back home, because I couldn't see a reason to take him to Eckhardt Lalor's funeral. I had a fake service dog halter I had used on him in the past when I wanted him to meet a suspect, but I didn't feel right doing that at a funeral.

As usual, he was eager to accompany me, and he looked mournful when I had to body-block him from getting out the front door. He'd sprawl out on the kitchen floor and watch for me through the sliding glass doors. He had figured out the particular angle that let him look through the gate to the driveway.

Once in a while, I'd park next door and creep up the driveway, trying to catch him snoozing. But he had that dog's special sense, and instead he would be sitting up on his haunches, staring at the gate, as if he'd been there all day.

I had a couple of cousins on my mother's side buried in Ewing Cemetery, so I'd been there before. It was behind the Trenton airport, in a neighborhood that still maintained a rural atmosphere despite its ease of access to I-295. I got to the cemetery just in time to see the parade of limos arrive, and as I watched people get out I figured out they'd gone with clan affiliations.

Jeffrey and Anita were first to arrive, with their spouses and children. I recognized him from a press photo, and I remembered that Melantha had said Jeffrey had given her daughter a good price on the Lalor home. I scanned his face for traces of kindness, or even sadness. Didn't get anything there. He was all business as he shepherded his tall, lanky son, and then Anita and her husband and son, toward the canopy.

Anita had the same strong jaw as her brother. She wore a simple black dress with a black lace shawl, and from her face she appeared to be the only one who cared about Eckhardt Lalor. Her husband was a square fellow about her age, and their son was surprisingly much older than Jeffrey's.

I wondered about that. Had she been the most eager to get out of her father's house? From what I intuited from the obituary, there must have been a time when she had to be the substitute mother to her brood of siblings, step-siblings and half-siblings. The easiest way to get out of that was to marry and set up her own household. And the sooner she had her own child, the less time she could be expected to spend with her father's.

Then Peter arrived in a large SUV with his blond daughter and son, and Jeffrey pulled Peter aside for a whispered conference. He looked like a younger, heavier version of his brother, though as I got closer I saw the spidered veins of a nascent alcoholic on his cheeks.

Their families milled around them, kids talking to cousins and aunts. Peter's younger daughter stood out, in a sharply patterned black and white dress with bright red accents the color of oxygen-rich blood, and matching red stiletto heels.

I wondered what Jeffrey and Peter were talking about. All three of the eldest siblings controlled the remnants of Lalor's property development and management business. The brothers pulled out their phones and it looked like they were comparing schedules, then making an appointment to meet.

Were they conspiring against their sister? Already? With their father not even buried yet?

I took a breath. I was making a very big leap. It was possible they were scheduling a golf game, or tickets to the Phillies.

The younger pair of Lalor's kids, Clifford and Elaine, were about my age, mid-forties. They arrived next, in a shared limo with their spouses and a rangy young man who had to be Clifford's son; they both had the same unruly curly hair.

The siblings hesitated at the curb, as if they didn't want to intrude on a private family event. But then Anita waved at them, and they trooped up to the chairs under the awning.

I was pleased to see that Jeffrey, Peter and Clifford all waited until their wives, sisters and kids were seated before standing to the side—Jeffrey and Peter to one side, and Clifford to the other. The family finances were evident in everyone's clothing. The older two brothers wore dark suits in a single-button style that fit them perfectly, down to exposing just the right length of shirt cuff beneath. The lace on Anita's shawl was so fine it looked like it had been created by nuns.

Clifford's suit looked like it came straight off the rack and had been worn more than a few times. A tell-tale thread dangling from one of the pockets indicated he'd never even cut open the threads that sewed the pocket shut. His brother-in-law, Elaine's husband, wore a gray sports jacket and black slacks. Their wives both had a similar straight-from-the-discount-store look.

To be fair, they might not have been anticipating a funeral, and had to scramble for something to wear. But if I was reading things correctly, there was a marked financial difference between the kids of Lalor's first wife and those of his second.

At the last minute, two more cars arrived. Susan, in a Toyota sedan, and last of all long-haired Robert in a panel truck with the name of his woodworking firm on the side. Both of them were alone. I saw Jeffrey scowl at them, and I wasn't sure if it was because they were late, or because they existed at all. Neither had bothered to dress up for the funeral. Susan wore what my mother would have called a dog dress, suitable for walking the dog, in a faded plaid pattern, and Robert wore jeans. At least he'd put on a collared shirt.

I remembered how Melantha had described those two after their mother's death, when they were orphans stuck with a stepfather and a bunch of step-siblings. I had to admit I was surprised to see them there.

A non-denominational minister appeared in a black suit, and led us through a couple of prayers. Then Jeffrey stepped up to speak. "My father was a pioneer in so many ways," he said. "He parlayed a small piece of inherited land in Trenton into a real estate empire that survives him today. In the early 1970s, he was one of the first to offer Section 8 housing to poor families in the city, providing them clean, safe places to live."

Robert snorted, and Jeffrey glared at him.

"He grew to be one of the largest operators of low-income housing in the city, but that wasn't enough for him. He opened up the countryside to build and sell houses to thousands of first-time homeowners. After our mother died, he took on the responsibility of being a single parent to my brother and sister and me. And if you know anything about our family, you know that was a Herculean task."

The audience chuckled. "When Dad met Jane, they merged their households in the manner of the Brady Bunch, and when Jane died suddenly, he was once more all alone, now in charge of seven children in a rambling house on Beachwood Avenue, and most afternoons he sent us all over to play in Cadwalader Park, with me and Anita in charge while he continued to work hard to support us."

I saw Anita dabbing at her eyes. "Then I went to college, followed the next year by Anita, and our housekeeper was promoted to the role of third wife, which she struggled with for a few years until she, too, left us. Dad got by on his own again with household help until Cliff and Lainey were ready to leave the nest."

I caught Elaine frowning at that. I'll bet she didn't like that nickname—and that she didn't much like Jeffrey either.

I noticed that he didn't mention Susan or Robert, his stepbrother and stepsister, by name, other than to lump them into the "seven children" left behind by their mother.

"Finally Dad transferred the operations of the business to me, and tried to enjoy some well-deserved rest. Sadly, Alzheimer's robbed him of that, and I had to take him into my home to keep tabs on him. But he loved to wander—whether it was walking the streets of Trenton in search of new property to buy, or just observing the natural world around Stewart's Crossing."

He wiped his eyes, though I hadn't seen any tears there. "Dad, here's hoping your wandering is at an end now, in God's comforting arms."

There was a murmur of appreciation, and Jeffrey sat down. "Does anyone else have anything to say?" the minister asked.

Surprisingly, Robert Nitz, Lalor's stepson, moved to the podium, though I could see Jeffrey and several of the other Lalors glaring at him. "We never called him Dad," he said, as he reached it. "He made that clear to Susan and me the day we moved in. We could call him Mr. Lalor or sir."

Another murmur through the crowd. It was hot under the tent, and many people fanned themselves. I stood out in the air, and a fresh breeze sweeping over the mixed array of tombstones.

"Maybe Jeff doesn't remember this, but when we used to go out to dinner as a group, then the bill came, Mr. Lalor always split it up. He paid for himself and his kids and my mother, but she had to pay for everything we ate. Jeff, Anita and Peter went to prep school in Princeton, but Susan and I went to Trenton High, even though it was one of the lowest rated schools in the state by then."

"Bitter much?" I heard Clifford mumble.

"And those Section 8 houses Jeff was bragging about? The city called them slums, and in a 1984 article the Trenton *Times* called Eckhardt Lalor the city's most prominent slumlord."

"That's enough," Jeffrey said.

"That's all I had to say anyway," Robert said, and stalked back down along the outside of the awning toward his truck. Susan dawdled for a moment, then stood up and followed him out.

The minister said a few more prayers and added, "The family will be receiving visitors at the home of Jeffrey Lalor in Stewart's Crossing this evening."

Two men from the funeral home began lowering the coffin into the ground. There were graves on either side of him, and I saw that the headstone was a triple one. In the center, Eckhardt Lalor's name took pride of place, and beneath it the year he was born.

To the left, and slightly below his name, was that of his first wife, Marie. At the same level and to the right was his second wife, Jane, mother to Robert and Susan, and then Clifford and Elaine with him. It made sense, though I wondered what his third wife, the one who had divorced him, had thought of that arrangement.

Seeing them in person made me realize that those last four were close in age, so that meant Robert and Susan must have been preschoolers when their father died. Jane and Lalor had then had two more babies quickly. That must have been tough on Jane—four kids under six years old, plus her three older stepchildren. No wonder Robert and Susan were bitter, if they'd been crowded into the middle of a family where their stepfather ruled.

Especially if, as Melantha had and Robert had said, Mr. Lalor was a tyrant.

The family moved back to their cars, and after hanging back a moment, I followed. Instead of heading home, though, I headed down Olden Avenue to Chambersburg, the neighborhood of Italian and Polish families. I had grown up on those streets, as my mother sourced Italian pastries and kosher meats, so I knew the area well, though I was surprised, as always, at how it had changed.

Saint Anthony's Catholic church was still there, reigning over the neighborhood, but its neighbors now included Guatepan Bakery and JNC African Hairbraiding. Gone was the little ice cream place where we got my birthday ice cream cake every year and the liquor store Uncle Lou's best friend owned, where we got "family prices."

Dog's Waiting Room

One of the first things Jews did when they moved to a new place, back in the old days, was establish a cemetery where they could be buried in hallowed ground. When my mother's father came to Trenton, he joined a group called the Workmen's Circle, a social group, and paid to join their cemetery. He and my grandmother were buried there, as were my parents.

I pulled up beside the iron gate and parked and scoped out my family plots. My mother, always on the lookout for a bargain, had snapped up the last pair in the cemetery, at the back corner, long before either she or my father got ill. I was pretty sure that was a direct response to her own mother's actions.

When my grandfather died, my Nana only bought one plot, for him. Maybe she was short of money, or maybe she figured she was young enough to marry again. In any case, by the time she died there was only one adjacent plot left—at my grandfather's feet.

My mother was determined she would be beside her husband, not at his feet. She had never thought, back then, that I might need a plot nearby.

As is our custom, I placed small stones on the corner of each headstone. And though I know the rules say you should only say the Kaddish, the prayer for the dead, in the presence of a minyan, a group of ten men, I disobeyed the law and recited the prayer in Hebrew. Under my breath, just in case the spirit of an angry rabbi buried nearby should overhear me and get upset. As I finished, a hot breeze swept over me and I hurried back to the air-conditioned car.

As I drove home, I thought about the bad feeling Rick had about Eckhardt Lalor's death, though the coroner had said it was accidental. Was it possible that he'd been pushed into the Delaware? Or had the footprints we'd found been the result of an accidental slide?

Many of the people clustered around the grave might have had a motive to see the old man dead—either for financial reasons or revenge for long-ago slights. But was his death murder? And if so, who'd given him the fatal shove?

Chapter 12
Wake Talk

Robert Nitz had aired his grievances and some of the family's dirty laundry at the funeral. Eckhardt had been a slumlord and a lousy stepfather. And Melantha had told me that Bobby and Susan had felt ignored by their stepfather when their mother died. But Robert was in his forties—surely he'd have gotten over being angry enough to kill.

It sounded like Lalor had been a wealthy man, and that could often be a source of friction. Wills could reveal deep divides within families, especially blended ones like Lalor's. From the way he spoke, I figured Robert wasn't expecting an inheritance from his stepfather. But what about the rest of them?

I called Rick and arranged to meet him at the Chocolate Ear café in downtown Stewart's Crossing. I got there first, and staked out a table in the front window, far enough from other customers that we could talk frankly, but still in the air conditioning.

It was a welcoming place in the middle of Main Street, with warm yellow walls and art nouveau posters of French food. I sat beneath one of a man in a tuxedo opening a bottle of champagne.

Rick must have walked to the café from his office in the police station, a few blocks away, because sweat was dripping down his forehead. He ordered an iced coffee, and when he got it, he held it up to his head.

"I went to Eckhardt Lalor's funeral today," I said, when he sat down across from me. "There was some family strife, but nothing out of the ordinary. Any idea what I should be looking at?"

"I spoke to Social Services right after Mr. Lalor died," Rick said. "When you found the old man wandering by the river, that triggered a welfare check. Jeffrey Lalor promised that he was going to keep his father under lock and key after that."

"Then how did he get out?"

"I wasn't allowed to ask. Once the death was ruled misadventure my ability to investigate went out the window."

"What does that mean exactly? Misadventure?"

"Basically that the deceased took the responsibility on himself for the risk of falling into the river." Rick fanned himself in the air conditioning, and some of the cold air rushed past me, too.

"But he had Alzheimer's," I said. "Doesn't that mean he wasn't capable of assessing the risk involved?"

"Jeffrey told the social worker the only thing wrong with his father was his memory, not his judgment. At least that's what she put in her notes."

"But you disagree."

"Wouldn't you? You met the man. What did you think?"

I sighed. "Honestly, Rick, I talked to him for all of about twenty minutes. Yes, he was confused and didn't seem to realize how he had gotten down there by the river. Yes, he had forgotten his name, but he remembered his son's, and he was compos mentis enough to realize that must be his name, too."

"I don't know. It seems too easy for me."

"The family are receiving visitors at Jeffrey's house tonight," I said. "I can go over there and pay my respects, see if I can figure anything else out. Though without Rochester..."

It felt weird not to have the golden by my side, but I'd had to leave him home because of the funeral. I missed having him there to listen to Rick, too. My golden has an uncanny nose for crime, and in the past he'd given me some useful clues.

Couldn't get them from him if he stayed home, though.

Lili was at a gallery opening in New Hope, so I drove home, where I fed and walked Rochester. When he saw me getting ready to go out again, he skittered across the tile floor to the front door, eager to go with me. I knelt down and ran my fingers through the golden ruff below his neck. "Sorry, puppy, I promise today is just an outlier. Tomorrow you can be by my side wherever we go."

I had adopted him after Caroline was shot to death while walking him, and that had made him more clingy and needy than most dogs, though I was sure he genuinely loved me.

He sat on his haunches and glared at me, and he tried to push through my legs when I opened the front door. It took a very solid "No!" to get him to step back and he stared at me with those big brown eyes as if I had wounded him deeply.

Crossing Estates, where Jeffrey Lalor lived, was a development of large two-and three-story homes, all with broad lawns and elegant landscaping. To get there I had to drive into town on Ferry Road, then turn north on Main Street for a couple of miles, until the one and two-story 1960s houses faded away, then past a couple of farms.

In the distance, I could see the field and hedgerow Eckhardt Lalor had walked past to get to the river. I stopped at the guardhouse to show my driver's license and explain where I was going. I'd been to the community a couple of times before. Most of the time, the guard had called the house to get permission to let me in. Once, however, Lili and I had gone to a holiday party, and the guard had checked us off on a list.

This time, he asked, "Going to see the family after the funeral?"

I nodded, and he opened the gate. As I drove in, I wondered if there were security cameras that might have caught Eckhardt Lalor taking off on his ramble. River Bend had such cameras, though they only focused on the cars and drivers.

Like River Bend, Crossing Estates was surrounded by rows of tall arborvitae trees that became a de facto fence. If you pushed hard enough, you could get in or out on foot. Rick had mentioned occasional burglaries out there, usually kids from poorer neighborhoods sneaking through the hedges. I imagined that if Lalor came out that way, he might have gotten scratched by the spiky branches.

Had his body exhibited such scrapes? I could have Rick ask the ME. But that didn't mean he got them from the arborvitaes. When I met him, he'd been scratched up and I assumed it was from the trees along the river.

Also like at River Bend, the homeowner's association took care of mowing lawns, and despite the recent summer rain the lawns were all uniformly manicured.

The rest of the landscaping was up to the homeowner, though, and I spotted a couple of massive oaks with broken branches, and a couple of places where the hedges needed a good trim. That was most evident at Jeffrey Lalor's house, where the azaleas under the windows had run rampant, and a scrawny pine by the side of the house was dropping needles at an alarming rate. It looked like the tree from the Charlie Brown Christmas special.

A flower bed along the fence between Lalor's house and his neighbor's was similarly untended, with barren places interspersed with flowers that needed to be dead-headed.

I had to park a block away from the Lalor house on Haviture Way because of all the visitors along the street. As I walked up, I heard a loud, throaty bark coming from the back yard. A dog who was not happy at being segregated back there, away from all the fun.

I paused in the driveway and gave the house a good look. The house needed a good paint job, too. There were big scrape marks along one side wall that looked like someone had moved a ladder sideways.

I flashed on a memory of my own father, who'd asked me to move a ladder for him when I was a teenager. I'd dragged it across the wall just like that. He had not been happy.

Security cameras were mounted on the garage, one aimed at the front door and one toward the street. Cameras like that operated on a low wi-fi network that let someone in the house see who was outside via an app on their cell phones or tablets.

Some archived their footage so you could scroll back a few days to see whose dog had pooped on your lawn, while others wrote over the footage every twenty-four hours.

The front door was slightly ajar, an invitation for everyone to walk in without being announced. As unobtrusively as I could, I surveyed the locks. There were two. The bottom lock was keyed inside and out, while the top lock had only a thumb turn on the inside.

From indoors you could turn the bottom lock open, too. So it was reasonable that even if Jeffrey thought he was keeping his father secure, Eckhardt could still slip out.

I entered a front foyer and saw the crowd in the living room to the left. I spotted the grieving siblings at various places around the room and considered who to approach first.

The decision was made for me when Anita came toward me. She was the middle child of the original three, and my experience of middle children had been that they were the empathetic peacemakers of the family. "I'm Anita Quinton," she said, offering me her hand. "Thank you for coming."

She wore the same black dress as at the funeral, though she'd put aside the black lace shawl.

"Steve Levitan," I said. "I met your father once, out along the Delaware." I shrugged. "My dog liked him, and he's a good judge of character. I wanted to stop by and express my condolences."

"Were you the one who called the police?"

There was a sharpness in her tone that I didn't appreciate.

"He didn't remember his name or address," I said. "He was tired and he looked dehydrated."

"I'm sorry for the way that sounded," she said. "We've had some problems with nosy neighbors calling social services when they saw my father outside. But I appreciate what you did." She sighed. "I only wish someone had been there the second time he got out."

"Was that only the second time?"

"Well, he'd gone wandering around the neighborhood before," she said. "Usually found his way home. Though once Jeff was driving home on River Road and spotted him trying to cross the road to the river."

She shook her head. "No matter how many times we talked to him and argued with him, it didn't make a difference. He was a stubborn man when he was healthy, and he was just as stubborn when he was sick. The difference is that he didn't recognize the danger he was in."

Her brother passed by, and Anita touched his arm. "Jeff? This is the man who found Dad down by the river."

"It was really my golden retriever," I said. "I had him off leash on the path, and he found your dad and barked to summon me."

"Goldens are wonderful dogs," Jeffrey said. "We had one growing up for a while. Right now we have an Akita. Thank you for looking after my dad."

"Did you and he live here on your own?" I asked. "Big house."

"My wife works for an Internet startup in Silicon Valley," he said. "She's out there a lot. My boy Noah is home from college for the summer. But you know how it is with kids. It was usually me and Dad. I do a lot of my work from home so it's not like we abandoned him."

"What do you do?"

"Same thing as Vivian. Internet startup. Though mine is nowhere near as successful as the place she works."

He saw someone else come in, thanked me again, and then left. "Can I get you something to eat or drink?" Anita asked.

"I can help myself. Thanks. I'm sure you have other people to speak to."

I wandered from group to group, trying to overhear anything useful. I made myself a ham sandwich with mayonnaise and got a glass of fruit punch, and snickered to myself about how different the food was from what I'd eaten in Miami after Benita's funeral.

Three young people were hanging out nearby, two boys and the girl with the red, white and black dress, though she had kicked off her heels and was standing barefoot.

"Did he give you a dollar for your birthday?" one boy asked the other. Both looked like they were college age.

"And at Christmas," the other one said. "Fresh and crisp, like he got a stack of them at the bank."

"I'm sure he did," the girl said. She had blonde hair like the first boy. "My father used to complain he spent fifty-five cents to mail us each a dollar."

"You think we'll get anything from his will?" the second boy asked.

The girl shrugged. "A stack of singles?"

"Maybe a roll of stamps, too," the first boy added.

"I could use some serious help with tuition," the second boy said. "My mom makes a ton of money in California, but the terms of her divorce from my dad says he has to pay for college. And I saw his FAFSA and he's broke."

"Uncle Jeff and Aunt Vivian are divorced, Noah?" the girl asked. "When did that happen?"

"A year ago. But my dad didn't want to upset Gramps so he didn't tell anyone. Just that my mom was working out there most of the time."

The girl looked up and noticed me, and I had to move along. I stood in the corner, finished my sandwich, and then walked out without speaking to anyone else.

Chapter 13
Security Camera

When I got into my aged BMW, I realized that my hacking laptop had slid up from under the front seat. I sat there looking at it for a couple of minutes, debating my next move. It was going to be illegal, but not harmful.

Then I picked it up. Fortunately, it had a charge. A couple of other visitors had left the Lalor house, so I was able to pull up the street and park a few inches from the edge of the driveway.

We'd had some incidents at River Bend a year before. Teenagers were roaming the streets after midnight, checking for unlocked cars, and stealing car chargers and handicapped decals. At that time I'd installed a security camera over my garage. We had a two-car driveway, but only one car could fit inside the garage, and often there was some bulk buy of paper towels or toilet paper blocking the way. So it was useful to keep an eye on the cars.

There was a motion sensor on the camera, and if I wanted to, I could check the digital photo captures from the night before through an app on my phone or laptop. I rarely did that, so my system archived footage for at least a month before writing over the hard drive.

It looked like the same model camera as I had, so I used the house's Wi-Fi (unsecured, dumb move for an Internet guy like Jeffrey) and downloaded the app. When asked for a username and password, I made some quick guesses.

Few people realize that those cameras can be hacked, so most don't bother with elaborate IDs and passwords. Jeffrey had used Lalor as the username, and the house number as the password.

I didn't want to spend too much time there because I didn't want to get caught by some family member leaving the wake, so I quickly downloaded the contents of the camera's hard drive to my laptop.

While I waited I felt my pulse rate start to accelerate. I'd gotten into the system so quickly that I hadn't considered the consequences. What would happen if Jeffrey Lalor or one of his siblings spotted me?

I put the laptop on the floor of the car and used my phone to check through messages and play a game or two. Innocent enough—I could say, if asked, I was killing time before I had to be somewhere.

And hope they wouldn't notice the activity on the laptop on the floor.

Jeffrey hadn't stinted on Internet speed, and the download was complete within minutes. I logged out, turned off the laptop, and drove home.

When I got there, Rochester romped up to the door to greet me, wagging his tail and barking. "I know, boy, I left you home twice today, and you don't like that."

One of the reasons I had taken the job at Friar Lake was that I could have Rochester with me every day. He loved to stay by my side in the office, and then to run around and chase squirrels and pee on bushes when I let him out.

We went for a long walk, and when we got back I sat down at my laptop and viewed the images the security camera had captured. I checked Eckhardt Lalor's obituary, and then started backwards from that date.

Lots of images of Crossing Estates security cars passing. Jeffrey going in and out, sometimes away from the house for hours. Anita Quinton visited the day before the obit appeared in the paper.

Dog's Waiting Room

And then, an image of Eckhardt being helped into the front seat of a car. The time and date stamp were only a few hours before his body was discovered in the Delaware.

Unfortunately, because of the angle of the camera and the interval between images, it wasn't clear who was with him.

I captured that image and used an anonymous email provider to create a message to the address for the chief of police in Stewart's Crossing, as well as the medical examiner. I wrote "Who took Eckhardt Lalor out in this car only hours before he drowned?"

I signed it, "A curious neighbor," and hit SEND.

Rochester was curled up under my feet, and Lili was still out at her gallery opening, so I started some research on Jeffrey and Vivian Lalor, to verify that they were divorced. For the official record, I had to contact the Bucks County Orphans Court Clerk and obtain a divorce record request application.

It was easier, though, to check the property appraiser's office. They had purchased the house in Crossing Estates five years before, for six hundred fifty thousand dollars. Six months before, a quit claim deed had been issued transferring the house into Jeffrey's name alone.

I checked online with the Bucks County Recorder of Deeds. To see if the house had a mortgage, I had to send a request and pay a dollar a page. I decided to be a sport and mail in a request.

Then I focused on Jeffrey and discovered that he had tried to start an anonymous social network the year before. He had apparently spent a lot of money on coding and hosting, trying to give people the safety that their posts would be restricted only to those they chose.

He overlooked what I considered the main point of a social network: social. If people didn't get a personal invitation to your account on Private.net, they couldn't find you. As a result, people's networks were small and ended up being used primarily for things like porn. Private.net had received a first and second round of angel investors, but when subscriptions didn't grow and there was little advertiser base, his investors had pulled the plug only three months before.

I was returning the laptop to its secure location in the attic when I heard Lili pull up. I finished what I was doing, replaced the ceiling panel, and I was carrying the ladder back to the garage when she walked in.

"Hey sweetie," I said, leaning in to kiss her cheek.

She smiled and said, "Hey," and then Rochester romped over to take all her attention. When I finished hanging the ladder from its hook on the garage wall, I found her sitting on the couch in the living room. I joined her there, and she kicked off her sandals and stretched out her legs. I reached into the cabinet by the sofa for the foot cream we kept there.

"You went to the funeral today," she said, as I uncapped the tube and squeezed some ointment into my hand. Rochester slumped on the floor, his head close to Lili's dangling right hand, and she stroked him.

"Yup, and the wake afterwards," I said. "A large and relatively dysfunctional family. And then I did a little research when I got home. Mostly legal, tracking down divorce and mortgages and so on."

"Mostly."

I massaged the cream into her left foot. I had promised Lili that I would keep my computer activities legal, and that if I ever crossed the line I would tell her, and Rick.

I explained about seeing the security camera over the Lalor garage, and how I'd been able to log into the camera's records using the company's app. "Honestly, if he wanted to secure his home, he should have used more than a common log in and password."

She raised her eyebrows. "Did you find anything?"

"I think so. A screen capture of someone walking the elder Mr. Lalor out of the house and into a car a couple of hours before he went into the Delaware." I paused. "Which means that most likely he did not leave the house under his own power and simply wander away."

"And what did you do with this evidence?"

Rochester looked up as if he recognized the word evidence, or maybe just Lili's tone. Then he slumped back to sleep again.

I kept massaging. She had a callus on the side of her left foot that bothered her sometimes. "I emailed it through an anonymizer to the chief of police and the medical examiner."

"Not Rick?"

"I wanted to keep him out of it for now. I signed it a curious neighbor. I think it's better for Rick to be surprised if the chief asks him to investigate."

"And if the chief doesn't?"

I looked up at her. "I don't know. He was a nice old man, friendly to Rochester, even if he wasn't as nice to his family. And he's dead, possibly at the hands of someone close to him. I'm not sure I can let that go."

"Keep rubbing. I was on my feet at that gallery too long." She peered at me. "When was the last time you had a haircut? You're looking kind of shaggy."

"I don't quite remember," I said. "But I can try and squeeze a cut in soon."

We were both quiet for a few minutes. Finally, she said, "I understand you, Steve. I know you have this need to be the white knight and bring justice to the world. Just promise me you'll be careful."

"Always," I said. "I promise never to do anything that could cause harm to you or Rochester."

"Or yourself," Lili said. "Now the right foot."

Chapter 14
Finding Lalors

The next morning I got a text from Rick as I was getting ready for work. *Need to see you ASAP.*

I called him back. "What's up?"

"Not on the phone. Chocolate Ear, half an hour?"

"I can make that."

On my way out of the house, I stopped to sniff the roses in the arrangement Adriano had sent. Nothing. I tried a couple of different blossoms but got the same result. All show, no scent. There was an analogy to be made to both Lili's exes, but I was too self-confident to make it.

Right.

When I got to the café, Rick was in the pet-friendly half, through a door from the part that sold food. He sat at a table under the air conditioning vents, intent on his phone. I dropped Rochester with him and went next door to order my coffee.

When I returned, with a biscuit for Rochester and a chocolate croissant for me, Rick looked up. "You really know how to set the cat among the pigeons."

It took me a moment. "Oh. Your chief got the email."

"Thank you, curious neighbor."

"You didn't tell him you knew who sent it?"

"I did not, because I wasn't a hundred percent sure, and I wasn't about to plunge myself into a pile of shit. Instead, he pushed me there."

"You mean he asked you to investigate."

He nodded, and I said, "Isn't that what you wanted?"

"I didn't want to have to interrogate every neighbor on the block," he said grumpily. "Do you know how hot it is?"

"Be careful what you wish for, pal."

He blew out a deep breath, and swigged more of his iced coffee, then used a napkin to dry his brow. "So I guess we're finally treating this as a murder case. You have anything else for me?"

"Jeffrey Lalor is divorced and broke," I said. "I can show you the records later. So he has a motive. I requested a copy of the will, but you can probably get that more quickly now that you have a case."

I agreed that I would do some research on each of the Lalor offspring, to see if I could identify motives. The only person we agreed could be eliminated was Vivian Lalor, who had not attended the funeral, and as far as we knew was living in California, though Rick said that he would verify that.

A couple of teenagers came into the café then, and Rochester sat up and nuzzled my hand. "You've already gotten your biscuit," I said to him. Then I looked at where his gaze was leveled, and added, "Good boy. We'll make sure to include all the grandchildren, as long as they're old enough to drive."

I leaned down and scratched behind his ears, and he grinned broadly. Or maybe that was because I had the skin from his face stretched out. Then he slumped back to the floor, his mission accomplished.

Rochester and I left Rick hunched over his phone making notes and drove up to Friar Lake. The big golden was delighted to reacquaint himself with all the familiar smells of his secondary domain, perhaps even noticing some new ones, if there were fresh squirrel droppings or the stray remains of a hawk's dinner.

Dog's Waiting Room

When things were slow that afternoon I did some research on the properties Lalor had owned. One property intrigued me. It was in West Trenton, far from where he usually invested.

It had been moved from Lalor's name to a revocable trust named 2-14-82 back in 1987. There was no indication in the real estate records why this particular property had been put into the trust, but I discovered that the real estate taxes on the property hadn't been paid for the last two years.

I checked in with Joey after that, and since things were slow I left around three o'clock and headed down the River Road. Rochester sat up and looked out the window when we bypassed the turn for River Bend. "A little detour on the way home, boy," I said. We crossed over the Scudder Falls Bridge and headed north again, relying on directions from my phone.

We made a quick right turn and began climbing a hill, and when we reached the Delaware Vue apartments, my phone told me we had arrived. Maybe it's because of my English degree, but I had an inherent distaste for fancy spellings like "Vue" instead of "View" and adding an unnecessary E to the end of the neighborhood called Delaware Pointe or the Sweet Shoppe in Levittown. What was wrong with Point? And I'd never consider living in the development outside Yardley called Autumn Colours. It seemed pretentiously British.

Hadn't we fought a war so that we didn't have to add extra U's to words?

Well, perhaps not for that specific reason. But still.

I pulled up in front of a two-story line of garden apartments. The entrance door was surmounted by a classical triangular pediment with two house numbers, one to each side. The buildings were pale yellow brick, with window air conditioners for each unit.

From the outside it looked much nicer than the typical places Lalor had owned in Trenton. Each apartment had a generously sized patio or balcony, and many were filled with floral baskets. The yards were neatly trimmed, the landscaping mature. Most of the parking spots were empty, as I expected if the people there worked all day, and those that remained were older model Japanese sedans with the occasional SUV or van.

Who lived there, and why had Lalor put the apartment in a trust? I parked a few buildings down from my destination and put Rochester on his leash. Then we stepped out of the car to do a reconnaissance.

Rochester did his usual sniffing of the ground, and selected a few shrubs to receive his anointment. Then he stopped and nuzzled something on the ground. I leaned down to see what it was and recognized it as a lottery-style gift card for one of the local restaurants, Fiddler's Creek Lodge. The idea was that you scratched the nine prize boxes, and if you matched three, you won that reward.

It hadn't been rained on, driven over or scratched off, so I put it in my wallet for later. As we continued down the street, a woman in her sixties or seventies pulled open the sliding glass door on a first-floor balcony, a few feet above the grass, and lit up a cigarette.

I had the uncomfortable sense she was watching us, probably to be sure that Rochester didn't poop somewhere, so I hurried him back to the car. It was only as we were driving past that I realized she was living in the unit owned by the trust Lalor had set up.

That didn't necessarily mean anything; she could be a tenant to whomever was the trust's beneficiary. But still I was sorry I hadn't gotten a better look at her.

When I got home, I opened up my regular laptop and called up the Mercer County Property Information portal. Nothing there except the name of the trust that owned the unit. I tried a couple of other legitimate ways to identify the beneficiary of the trust, but came up empty-handed each time.

It irritated me. This was why people like me hacked into computer systems. Because the information we wanted was behind a firewall, required a password we didn't have, or otherwise locked us out.

Back in 1994, at the first Hackers Conference in Marin County,

California, Stewart Brand, who edited the *Whole Earth Catalog,* had stated, "Information wants to be free." It was a truth I had subscribed to for a long time – until it put me in prison. But I still believed that the vast majority of information locked up had no need to be. Why couldn't I know who the beneficiary of the 2-14-82 trust was?

It reminded me of the old-fashioned padlocks with a dial you spun. Turn right twice and stop at two, then left twice to 14, then forward to …82. Only a padlock usually didn't have that many numbers on it.

Was it the combination to a safe? A birthday or anniversary? It taunted me, like a Rubik's cube with the colors out of line.

Rochester must have sensed my frustration, because he came over to see me, his big golden tail swishing, and he knocked over a pile of greeting cards Lili had brought home from her mother's house and left on the coffee table. I got up to pick them up, and Rochester nuzzled me.

"What is it, boy? Haven't I been paying enough attention to you?"

A couple of the cards were ones that Lili had sent her parents from far-off places. One of them was titled *Feliz Aniversario* and showed two adorable puppies kissing each other.

Ha. So Lili had been a dog lover all along! And of course Rochester would pick that card among all the others.

Something itched at my brain, though. The name of the trust was 2-14-82. Could that stand for February 14, 1982? Would that particular Valentine's Day have any meaning to Eckhardt Lalor?

I went back to my computer with an idea. The state of New Jersey wanted me to register, pay a fee and wait to get a copy of a marriage license, but I subscribed to a couple of less demanding sites, willing to serve up the information I needed immediately. And sure enough, on February 14, 1982 Eckhardt Lalor and Genevieve Ehret had been married.

Was that Genevieve Ehret Lalor I had seen on that patio?

An hour later, Lili sent me a text. *Lots of paperwork from Fedi. Staying at work late to sort through it.*

I replied, *I need to see Rick anyway. Will feed the hound & bring you dessert.*

She responded with a couple of heart emoticons and one of a slice of cake, so I knew my assignment.

I called Rick and told him that I had some information for him. "You free for dinner?"

"As it happens, I am. Tamsen's out all day listening to a motivational speaker tell her how to sell more knickknacks and Justin's already scheduled for an after-school and dinner at Hannah's."

We agreed to meet at six-thirty at The Drunken Hessian, the bar slash restaurant in the center of Stewart's Crossing. I wished I could take Rochester with me, but a bar has been in that location since the 1700s and it hasn't been updated all that much since then—though the owners did install indoor plumbing at some point. Certainly no special area for dogs, the way there was at the Chocolate Ear.

Before I met with Rick, though, I had to research the two Lalor orphans. I found Robert Nitz easily, because he was a handyman in Levittown, the huge sprawling neighborhood centered around the now defunct US Steel Fairless Works plant—and not far from where Rick and I had gone to high school.

He had a website under the name "Levitt-To-Me Handyman," with a cell phone number and numerous testimonials from satisfied clients. A quick scan did not show any from family members.

Contrary to sense, Levittown was not a city of its own but instead spread over forty-one residential sections, under the jurisdiction of three townships and one borough. I couldn't find any property in his name, and when I opened one of my paid databases to track him, it seemed like he moved around a lot. Most of the addresses listed under his name appeared to be rental apartments in grim corners around the Oxford Valley Mall and along Route 13, an area of properties like the ones his stepfather had owned in Trenton.

On instinct, I turned to a database of criminal records that I had

Dog's Waiting Room

access to and Robert Nitz popped up quickly. A list of drunk and disorderly charges in Tullytown Borough and the three townships. A case of criminal mischief a few years before, never brought to trial.

Robert was significantly lower on the economic scale than the Lalors. However, his speech at the funeral indicated that he and his sister had always been treated as outsiders, so I doubted they'd have much expectation of an inheritance.

But then, sometimes money had nothing to do with death, and old grievances that might have been long since buried could rise up to the top with the slightest provocation. Had Robert Nitz been in contact with his stepfather? He had a history of violent acts while drunk. I could see him picking up his stepfather, manhandling him into a vehicle, and then driving him down to the river.

That was all speculation, though. I had only seen him once, at the funeral, and hadn't spoken to him.

The youngest step-sibling was the hardest to find. Susan's husband hadn't been named in the obituary, and I couldn't find any social media profiles under Susan Nitz. I finally turned back to the paid search engine, because it made connections between family members and people who resided at the same address.

Sure enough, an address for Susan Nitz popped up in Hammonton, New Jersey, at the edge of the Pine Barrens. Five other names were connected to her, a mix of male and female, so I couldn't tell if they were all roommates, or if one of them was her life partner.

Further searching turned up nothing that matched any of the five. No marriage licenses, no phone numbers, no social profiles. I made a note that I wanted Rick to find out as much as he could about Robert and Susan as he began interviewing the siblings.

Before we left Friar Lake, I let Rochester have a good long run on the bright green grass, dappled with shade from the towering oaks and maples. I'm an experienced dog dad, after all. He'd conk out as soon as he had his dinner, and I wouldn't have to feel guilty leaving him while I went to meet Rick.

The air conditioning in the bar was cranked up to maximum, but it was June and there were lots of sweaty revelers crammed inside. When I was growing up in the Lakes neighborhood of Stewart's Crossing, we had one window air conditioner in my parents' bedroom, and an exhaust fan in the ceiling to move air through the rest of the house.

I spent a good chunk of my childhood summer in the library in the center of town, slumped in a chair and lost in Narnia, ancient Wales, or post-war Britain beside Miss Marple or Hercule Poirot. We had central air installed when I was a teenager, so I could keep reading in my own bedroom.

A lot of the older houses in town still relied on window units—hence the crowd at the bar. I found Rick in a wooden booth toward the back, surrounded by the scratchings of thousands of patrons before us. He already had a pitcher in front of him and a pair of glasses, so I slipped into the booth and poured myself a beer.

"What are we drinking?"

"As soon as the server said she had Dogfish Head on tap I stopped her and ordered a pitcher. Tastes like an ale."

He lifted a glass and I did too, and as they clinked he said, "Thanks for a hot day in the sun."

"Oh, please. You love investigative footwork."

The server came back and we ordered steaks and baked potatoes. Looking at the crowd, I had her put aside a slice of their special chocolate cake to go, too.

"What did you come up with?" I asked Rick when the server had gone.

Rick pulled a bright blue notebook out of his shirt pocket. As usual, it had the imprint of some company I'd never heard of. Tamsen picked up all kinds of samples from her advertising specialties trade shows.

"Not much. Suburban neighborhood like that, most men work in New York or Philly. If there are small kids, there's a nanny or the wife is busy all day keeping tabs on them. Two different women, though, told me they had seen Eckhardt Lalor walkabout in the neighborhood during the day over the past month. And one delightfully gossipy woman down the block filled me in on the whole Lalor story, most of which you already know."

He sipped his beer. "Moved in about five years ago, everything was fine. Then about a year ago things started to go to pot. Lalor fired the regular landscaping service and neighbors began to complain to the management office about overgrown bushes. Soon after that, the wife moved out, but the boy stayed. He was a senior at Pennsbury High and didn't want to go."

He looked up. "At least that's what he told Mrs. Crown's daughter, who was in his class. He went to college in California, I guess to be near his mom. School called Harvey Mudd. You ever hear of it?"

I nodded. "The most expensive college in the country. Part of a loose affiliation called the Claremont Colleges. Maybe an hour east of LA."

"The mother is in Palo Alto, but that's near San Francisco. Think he couldn't get into Stanford?"

"Possibly not. I think it's one of the top ten most competitive. Though I don't think Harvey Mudd rates that much farther down the list. And if you think about the timing, he'd have been accepted to college some time before his parents broke up."

It was my turn to sip my beer while I thought. "I have a feeling I overheard him at the wake. Noah, right?"

Rick nodded.

"He and his cousins were complaining about how cheap Grandpa was—a crisp dollar bill for birthdays and Christmas."

Rick laughed.

"And Noah said that he needed money for tuition this fall. That the terms of the divorce say his dad has to pay for his college, but he's broke, and his mother makes too much for him to get financial aid."

He added that to his notes. "No one I spoke to was home the day that Eckhardt Lalor drowned," Rick said. "One of our tech guys enhanced that picture of Lalor getting into the van, but we couldn't see enough detail to establish make or model. You have anything else?"

I shook my head. "Only that one shot on the camera's hard drive. It's set up to take a single shot each time it detects motion."

"What about coming home? There has to be a shot of the vehicle returning, right?"

"The only car that returns is Jeffrey Lalor's," I said. "And that doesn't prove anything, because he lives there and he could be coming home from anywhere. If he's guilty, and smart, he'll have stopped off for groceries or something on the way home so he has an alibi for the general time of death."

"The ME was happy, by the way. The time stamp on the photo helped him narrow the time of death window considerably."

He looked at me. "What have you got for me?"

I sat back against the hard wood of the booth. This was going to take a while.

Chapter 15
Trust

"I drove out to West Trenton today to find the apartment that Lalor put into a trust," I said. "I think I might have seen his ex-wife there."

He picked up his glass and took a swig. "You think?"

"I saw a woman on the patio of the apartment, smoking a cigarette. I haven't seen a photo of the ex-wife so I had nothing to compare it to."

"What drew you out there?" he asked.

"I did some research. The name on the trust is odd, 2-14-82. It had to mean something, and I snooped around, all legally, or at least all information I can get without breaking in anywhere." I stopped. This was where Rochester came in, and if I'd been talking to anyone other than Rick I'd have glossed it over.

"I was baffled, trying to figure out what the combination of numbers meant. And then Rochester came over to me looking for love, and his big tail swiped a bunch of cards off the coffee table. Cards Lili had sent her parents for their anniversary."

"And?"

"It came to me. I wondered if it was an anniversary, and when I looked up the records, I realized that that's the day that Lalor married a woman named Genevieve Ehret."

"That was his third wife?"

"Yup. The one who was 'promoted' from housekeeper, but who only lasted for a few years. I haven't been able to get a copy of the divorce, though."

"I can work on that."

"Also whatever you can find on Lalor's adopted daughter, Susan Nitz. She has zero online profile, other than a single address I really had to hunt for. I can keep digging, but..."

"But we'd both rather get the information legally," he finished. "I'll put both women on my list. In the meantime, I need your research skills. Tomorrow I start talking to the family members and I'd like a few pointed questions to ask." He yawned. "And I'm too beat from canvassing all day to do much homework."

"Yeah, I get it. Put me on the guilt train."

The server brought our steaks, sizzling, with oversized Idaho potatoes brimming with butter, sour cream and bacon bits. I inhaled once and my taste buds went wild, even though from experience I knew the food wasn't going to taste as good as it looked.

We ate in silence for a couple of minutes, and then I said, "If you can give me until noon, I'll put together a brief bio for you on all the siblings and look for any red flags."

"That's fine. I need to write up my notes from today anyway. We have new efficiency forms we have to fill out to make sure we're using our time effectively. I have to identify the reason behind each interview, the time it takes, and the results. Then pass all the forms to some computer wonk who comes back and says I'm taking too much time talking to grieving widows or interviewing suspects with nothing to say."

"Not to mention the amount of time spent filling out forms."

"Please don't mention it." He pulled a manila envelope from the seat next to him. "You didn't get this from me. But I knew that if I didn't get you a copy you'd find one on your own, and I don't want that."

I started to open it, and he said, sharply, "Not here. Wait til you get home."

"Fine." I put the envelope down beside me, though my fingers itched when I did. I really wanted to know what was inside, but it was clear Rick didn't want to discuss it at the Drunken Hessian.

We finished our dinner and I picked up the chocolate cake for Lili and drove home. I got home safely; I'd kept my Dogfish Head consumption within reasonable limits, and not just because I was sitting across from a cop. I remembered years when I lived in New York, going out on binges with my grad school roommate Tor, when we'd share pitcher after pitcher of cheap beer, filling up on bar nuts and pretzels. It never mattered what condition we were in when we left the last bar; neither of us had a car in the city, and we could almost always wake up and be functional the next morning.

I had never been in danger of alcoholism—my addictive tendencies were more of the computer kind than anything I ingested. I did drink a lot more during Mary's bad periods, but I never blamed my hacking on tequila, though Jose Cuervo was a friend of mine.

When I got home, Rochester was all over me, barking and licking like I'd abandoned him. But I had to see what was in the envelope Rick had handed me.

I sat on the sofa, and Rochester clambered up beside me as I opened the clasp on the envelope.

Rick had photocopied Eckhardt Lalor's last will and testament for me.

Now who was operating on a slippery slope? I was pretty sure it was against police regulations for him to have copied that document for me. There must be something in it he wanted me to see.

I only had time to glance at it, though, before Lili came home. When he heard Lili's car in the driveaway, Rochester jumped over me like I was one of those yellow speed bumps and rushed for the door. I harnessed him for his last walk of the day. Because he was pulling on me all I had time for was a quick kiss and, "The cake's in the fridge."

By the time we returned, only crumbs remained on the plate in front of Lili. "I needed that," she said.

I slipped into the chair across from her. "Bad time with your brother?"

"Not his fault. There's so much paperwork. My mother had six separate investment accounts. At six different brokers, with different log-ins and passwords and rules for inheritance."

"Wow. Six?"

"Don't get too excited. Most of them had only twenty or twenty-five thousand in them. According to Fedi, she'd get these offers to earn extra money for a deposit of new money, and she'd move the required minimum in and then forget about it."

"Nice to be able to do that," I said. My father had left me a little cash along with the townhouse, and through judicial investment I'd multiplied it until it was a comfortable emergency account. But I couldn't imagine moving twenty grand at a time.

"Nice for her, maybe," Lili grumbled. "Poor Fedi. Remember we left him that huge folder of bank statements? He has to go through each company and arrange to get the money out. Copies of the death certificate, copies of the will. Notarized copies of the distribution forms. And because the will says we get everything equally I can't just say Fedi, you take account X and I'll take account Y."

"I'm sorry you have to go through so much."

"At least Juanita in Accounts Payable is a notary," she said. "I'll have to buy her department a cake or give her a bottle of wine or something."

"I've been to the AP office," I said. "The walls are pretty barren there, aren't they, except for some legal notices? Why don't you frame some of your photos of the Eastern campus for them, too?"

"You think they'd like them?"

"Sweetheart, you're an amazing artist. You draw so much emotion out of your subjects. There's that one shot you did, of the graduation parade going past Fields Hall? It makes me swell up with pride whenever I see it."

"You're sweet."

"Trust me. A cake is a good start, but a couple of photos for the walls will liven up their workspace and make them happy to see you whenever you need something."

"Spoken like a true college bureaucrat," she said. "And I mean that in the nicest possible way."

"I'm not sure there is a nice way to call someone a bureaucrat," I said, but I smiled.

Chapter 16
Legacies

There was no time after that to go back to Eckhardt Lalor's will, but I carried the manila envelope with me to Friar Lake on Thursday morning. Once there, I dispensed quickly with my college business. Then I opened the envelope again.

This time I read through it carefully, and I was crushed to see that there was no big honking motive jumping off the page. If anything, I was surprised at how generous Lalor had been.

It began with a statement that the bulk of his wealth had already been distributed amongst his three oldest natural children, who owned equal shares in JAP Investments. He asked his executor to liquidate his remaining investments, either in property or financial instruments, and distribute the proceeds as directed.

There was no indication there what the total value of his estate was, but the list began with bequests to his two younger natural children, Clifford and Elaine, of $150,000 each. His two adopted children, Robert and Susan, each received $75,000.

Not chump change, and probably more than Robert and Susan were expecting, given the glacial distance between them and Eckhardt.

Each of his natural grandchildren were to receive $25,000.

Jeffrey's son Noah, Anita's kids Jennifer and Marc, Peter's kids Jackson and Amelia, and Clifford's son Cody. That was a lot of crisp dollar bills, though it wouldn't go very far towards Noah's tuition at Harvey Mudd.

There were no kids mentioned for either Robert or Susan, either because they didn't exist, or because Lalor didn't know about them. It was always a possibility that he'd shut them out, too.

Any personal effects were to be sold or donated to charity, with funds added to the estate. Several pieces of antique Lenox porcelain, originally collected by his first wife, were to be donated to the Trenton Historical Society in his name, along with any residue after his bequests. If funds allowed, he wanted a plaque to be placed at Ellarslie describing his family history in the Trenton area.

There might be some surprises in the will—perhaps Jeffrey, Anita and Peter expected more, as Clifford and Elaine might have, and Robert and Susan could be surprised to be included at all. But what if one of them knew the contents, and needed the money?

There was a single trust mentioned, the one I had found record of, and Jeffrey was appointed trustee. The will directed him to the conditions of the trust, and that once those conditions were satisfied he was to dissolve the trust and share the proceeds equally among his four natural siblings and his two adopted siblings.

I doubted that small condo would fetch much money, and thought it was perhaps less generous of Lalor and more a stab at forcing Jeffrey to deal with his family.

Since I had nothing pressing on my calendar, I began gathering information about each of the Lalor siblings, as I had promised Rick I would do.

Most of it was fairly straightforward. They all lived in either Bucks County, which encompassed Stewart's Crossing and a lot of other towns, or Mercer County, the corresponding one across the Delaware. All I had to do was put in Lalor on the respective property appraiser websites to start collecting data.

There wasn't as much as I expected. Jeffrey's place in Crossing

Estates was far more expensive than any of the properties owned by his siblings. Anita and Frank Quinton lived in a solidly middle-class neighborhood in Hamilton Township, a suburb of Trenton. They had bought the house twenty years before for just under two hundred thousand dollars.

Peter Lalor owned a condo in the trendy Mill Hill neighborhood of Trenton, not far from the street named for his family. He'd been there for close to ten years. Like his sister, it didn't look like he was living above his means, since he was a bureaucrat for the city of Trenton and I was able to establish he had an annual salary of $90,000.

I was idly following links when I stumbled on a newspaper article about Anita's daughter. The headline was "Hamilton Woman Victim of Suicide," and I nearly missed it because the woman in question was named Jennifer Q. Zale. But perhaps because I was in a gray mood, I kept reading.

The article was dated in mid-January of 2014. The journalist had done an in-depth interview with Jennifer's husband William. "'She was only thirty-one,' William Zale said when we met at the couple's apartment in the shadow of the I-195 expressway. 'And other than a miscarriage in late November, she was in good health.' He leaned forward. 'The doctor said she was suffering from depression, and he prescribed her some pills.'

"Some evidence suggests that Selective Serotonin Reuptake Inhibitors [SSRIs] may cause worsening of suicidal ideas in vulnerable patients," the article continued. "Mr. Zale wanted to convey this information to friends and family of those suffering from depression and considering suicide. "'I thought she was getting better,' he told me. 'She was getting up, getting dressed, going out for walks.'"

The article continued, "Police determined she drove to Trenton, parked her car in the New Jersey State Museum lot, then walked to the Calhoun Street bridge."

I knew that bridge well—it was the conduit between Trenton and Morrisville on the Pennsylvania side of the Delaware.

"She had a large quantity of sedatives as well as most of a bottle of bourbon in her system by the time she jumped into the rocky river below. She suffered numerous injuries on impact, and drowned before a rescue team could reach her."

The article ended with Mr. Zale entreating physicians to exercise care in prescribing the medication Jennifer had been taking, and with her survivors, her parents, Frank and Anita Quinton of Hamilton Township and her brother, Marc Quinton of Philadelphia.

I sat back in my chair, and Rochester came over and rested his head on my knee. I stroked his golden head as I thought about Jennifer Zale's tragic suicide. My ex-wife Mary had coped with her first miscarriage through retail therapy, rather than anti-depressants. I had been so busy working extra hours to pay for all Mary's expenses that I'd never had time to process my own feelings.

Then she had miscarried a second time, and I jumped into action. Between my job at the time, writing computer security manuals, and some exploration on my own, I'd developed some hacking skills, as well as the knowledge of where to find dangerous code I wasn't capable of writing myself. And so I'd hacked into the three major credit bureaus and put a flag on Mary's accounts.

I'd been caught, and spent a year in prison. I still bore the scars of that loss and the consequences of my actions. I could only image how bad Anita Quinton and her son-in-law felt. Then add that to both Jennifer's and Eckhardt's deaths involving the river.

Something in me jerked awake at that. Both deaths were connected to the Delaware. Was that the only link between them, besides the family lineage? Jennifer couldn't have killed her grandfather; the timing was wrong. I wasn't an estate attorney, but the money intended to Jennifer should have reverted to the estate, and I couldn't see that small an amount being worth killing her for.

Jennifer had been a CPA in private practice and I found a reference to her website, ZaleCPA.com. The site was defunct, though, and the URL was up for sale.

I turned to the Wayback Machine then. A digital archive of the

Dog's Waiting Room

World Wide Web, it proved that nothing you put up was ever gone, even if you took it down. I remembered the original, a time travel device used by Sherman and Mister Peabody in the animated cartoon *The Adventures of Rocky and Bullwinkle and Friends*.

I went to the site and entered the URL. The ZaleCPA site had been changed eighteen times between its origin years before and the take-down a few months previously. I clicked on the first available snapshot, taken six years before. The first image that popped up was of a pretty young woman who wore her hair the same way as Anita Quinton.

From her bio, I learned that Jennifer had graduated from Rutgers Business School in 2004 with a major in tax accounting and passed her CPA exam that fall with one of the highest scores in the state. She had immediately begun work for Ernst & Young as a tax services assistant manager in their Hoboken, NJ office, providing specific tax technical services to US and global clients.

After four years there, she had opened her own tax practice in Hamilton, New Jersey. Her client list included a number of local businesses: a hair salon, a tae kwon do studio, a pharmacy and a chiropractor.

And JAP Investments, a New Jersey-based real estate investment and management firm. The one organized by her grandfather, her mother and her uncles.

I used the Wayback Machine to check for each new snapshot of Jennifer's website. She had spoken to the Kiwanis and the Elks about tax planning. She had joined the board of a small private school in Lawrenceville.

The last time her site had been edited was in early December of 2013, when she posted a list of end-of-year tax planning tips. There were no more snapshots after that.

After jumping around between social media sites I figured out that Jennifer and William had become pregnant in September of 2013, and begun sharing details about the upcoming birth soon after that. Sadly, I knew that most miscarriages happen in the first trimester before the 12th week of pregnancy.

Social media posts stopped abruptly right before Thanksgiving, and that's when Jennifer must have suffered her miscarriage. From the interview with her husband, it seemed like she had lost interest in work soon after that.

That was awkward for a young, self-employed tax professional. She should have been busy advising her clients about the kind of end-of-year planning she had posted on her website. Though maybe that was her way to get the information out without having to meet with or talk to her clients.

Was she working for JAP then? Was it possible that she'd found something unusual in the records of the family business, and that had contributed to her depression? What could that be?

And more important, would it give William Zale a motive for vengeance against his late wife's family?

Chapter 17
Property Values

I checked the clock; it was only eleven in the morning, so I still had an hour to go before I'd promised some material to Rick. I went back to the computer.

Clifford and his family lived in Lawrenceville, on the prosperous side of Trenton, and from Facebook I saw that they also owned a condo at the Jersey shore, in Lavalette. Neither property looked that fancy in photos. He was an assistant vice president of patient care for the Capital Health hospital system. According to his employee profile, he had a bachelor's degree in biology from Rutgers and a master's in Health Service Administration from one of the big online universities.

And yet he didn't own a suit, or at least not one suitable to wear to his father's funeral. What was up with that?

His sister Elaine was the only one who didn't own property. She lived in a garden apartment complex in Ewing Township and was a self-employed book editor and manuscript consultant. She had been an editor for a big press in New York and had set up her own shingle two years ago.

I wondered if she had money problems and was expecting an inheritance from her father.

I turned to Rochester. "You think we should swing past the places where Clifford and Elaine live and see if we can discover anything?"

He lay down on the ground, his head resting on his paws so I couldn't see his eyes. "I figured out that Jeffrey was in financial trouble when I saw the poorly-kept landscaping around his house, didn't I, boy?"

Usually Rochester is eager to jump up and head for the car. But this time he resisted, and I looked down at his head, golden hairs shining in the morning light. Both the youngest Lalors had jobs and were living well under the standard their eldest brother had set.

"I know, you're right," I said to him. "Skulking around their homes might easily be considered stalking. It was different in the other cases—I'd been quasi-invited to Jeffrey's after the funeral, and I hadn't known who lived in the condo owned by the trust."

This kind of invasion of privacy was something I'd had to consider after the hacking incident. I had convinced myself that I didn't do anyone harm—that the only person affected had been my own wife, and all I did was try to protect her from her own impulses.

But then, as I continued to do a bit of illicit computer work after my release, I had to draw a line somewhere. I couldn't let myself do something to harm someone else, even if that person was a criminal. It was up to society to exact punishment. All I could do was provide proof of bad actions. In doing so, I wasn't harming the criminal, merely bringing his or her actions to light.

And if that led to punishment? Well, that was out of my hands. At least that's what I told myself, and it was the reason why I couldn't go snooping around the houses of people who not only might be innocent, but had also suffered a loss.

The alarm I'd set on my phone dinged to remind me it was quarter to twelve. I quickly reviewed all the notes I'd made, and organized them by sibling, with pertinent questions at the end of each chunk. I also asked Rick if he could find out who had taken over preparing the taxes for the family firm with Jennifer Zale's death.

Dog's Waiting Room

Then, just as my computer's clock was ticking from 11:59 to 12:00 I hit "send" and the information went winging its way to Rick.

Suddenly Rochester jumped up and rushed out of my office and into the small lobby area that had been built as a waiting room for guests. I admit I freaked out a bit—suppose President Babson was making one of his unplanned visits? What could I tell him I'd been doing all morning?

I was trying to think fast as Rochester sniffed at the door. Then my heart rate settled when Joey opened it.

Chapter 18
Soul-Crushing

"I was thinking," he said, as he walked in. "You're going to be here on Saturday, right? So if you want to take off tomorrow you can. There's nothing going on."

"I just took a week of personal leave," I said.

He shrugged as he sat down in the chair across from my desk. "Nobody but us has to know. And besides, you'll be making it up on Saturday."

"I see your point." Neither of us filled out time sheets, but the college did give us a limited number of sick days, personal days and vacation days, and we were expected to enter them into the HR mainframe. I usually didn't bother if either Joey or I took off an afternoon or came in late one morning, because the time always evened out in the end.

Rochester, who loved Joey almost as much as he loved me, sat beside Joey and sniffed his knee. Although the affection might have been simply his searching for information on Joey's white golden retriever, Brody. I did see a few white hairs on Joey's jeans.

"I might do that," I said. "I've been working on something with my friend Rick, and I could use the time to do some on-the-ground research."

"Another dead person? I mean, beyond Lili's mother?"

I nodded. "Property developer in Trenton. Retired, living with his son in Crossing Estates. Drowned in the Delaware."

"Mr. Lalor?"

"You knew him?"

He stretched out his legs, and Rochester settled beside him, sniffing his shoes. "When I was a teenager, I did construction work during the summers. A buddy and I worked on a Lalor project in Trenton for a while. Converting this big old mansion on Prospect Street into apartments."

"How was it?"

"Honestly? Kind of soul-crushing. I loved those old buildings, all the elegant craftsmanship that went into them. He had us rip out this beautiful crown molding so you couldn't tell he'd made smaller rooms out of big ones. And the new stuff we put in? Strictly second-rate, barely to code. I hated it but I stuck it out for a summer because my dad wouldn't want me to quit."

That was Joe Sr., who had been in charge of the physical plant at Eastern, and had brought Joey on to supervise the construction of Friar Lake. "Glad you didn't quit here," I said.

"This place was the exact opposite. Remember my dad let me drive down to that quarry in Coatesville to match the stone to repair the dining hall?"

I did. One wall had crumbled, and we'd considered replacing it with lath and plaster, but Joey had advocated for stone.

"So Lalor was a cheapskate," I said.

"More than that. It was like he never wanted to consider that real people were going to live in these apartments. I remember the super had a big argument with him over the lead pipes. There was already evidence that lead was leaching out into the water, and the super wanted to replace everything with PVC."

"How'd that work out?"

"The super reported it to the building inspector. The inspector made the removal of the lead pipe a requirement. And as soon as the work was done Lalor fired the super."

"Jerk move."

"Sure was. I was glad to be out of there." Joey stood up. "So I'll see you Monday. I'll do a solid check of all the recreational areas before I leave today and fix anything I find."

I thanked him, and made a note of his impressions of Lalor. Then I went back to my research. I shifted my focus to those too long dead to worry about any investigation. My mother grew up in Trenton, and many of the people she knew moved south of the city after the riots in 1967 destroyed the Battle Monument area in the center of town. The easiest way for us to reach those folks was to take the Calhoun Street Bridge to Route 29, which scoured a path through what had been the old Jewish neighborhood along the river.

That, I remembered, was the bridge where Jennifer Quinton Zale had taken her life.

My mother and I – always my mother and I, because on the weekends my father rested, unless he was dragged to some family event—would turn inland at Lalor Street, which ran along the side of downtown to South Broad Street, Route 206, which led south and east. Since Lalor was such an important street, I wondered if had been named after a local landowner or other important person.

I found a pedigree that went back to Tipperary in Ireland. A Jeremiah Lalor had settled in New Brunswick, New Jersey, and been a merchant there. He married a woman named Kitty de Klyn, daughter of an early settler in Brooklyn who went on to become a prominent landowner in New Jersey. They had a number of children; the oldest was his father's namesake.

Upon Jeremiah's death in 1807, at the relatively youthful age of 42, Kitty, a mother of seven, remarried John Beatty. He was a doctor, a veteran of the Revolutionary War, and had been a delegate to the Continental Congress in 1784 and 1785.

By the time of his marriage to Kitty, he was the president of the

Trenton Trust Company – a bank that was still in existence when I was a kid, and where my mother banked.

When his grandfather de Klyn died, Jeremiah Lalor Jr. inherited three hundred acres of land on the outskirts of Trenton—right where Lalor Street ran.

I had been through the area on my way home from the funeral, and I was surprised that it seemed more vibrant than it had when I was a kid. Some chain stores and restaurants had popped up, and a couple of new apartment buildings had been built. Did Lalor's company still own anything there?

Rochester rolled over onto my foot, and I had to move my chair. "I know, boy, this isn't the most exciting information, and it doesn't directly relate to Eckhardt Lalor. But you know me, I can get lost in research."

He agreed by sitting up so that I could pet him.

I did. "Suppose I fast-forward to whenever Lalor first started assembling his slum empire," I said. Rochester rolled back over onto the floor and I was able to put both hands on the keyboard. The property appraiser's office was of little help; their digitized records didn't go back that far. So I logged into the Eastern College library and began trolling through their databases.

The Trenton *Times* had a digital archive, and Eastern subscribed to it. I was able to log in using my employee ID and search for Eckhardt Lalor.

Thousands of results popped up—most of them having do with something happening on Lalor Street. Rookie mistake; I went back and put "Eckhardt Lalor" in quotation marks.

A much more manageable list of about two hundred results popped up.

Some I was able to dismiss quickly—reports of who had attended meetings, where Lalor's name was one among many. He had a penchant for social and networking organizations; he supported the Big Brothers and Big Sisters of Mercer County and the YMCA, and belonged to the Kiwanis, the Rotary, and the Lions as well as the Elks Lodge and the Loyal Order of Moose.

His interest was not always charitable, I was sure. Many government officials belonged to those groups, and if he needed a zoning change, or a problem resolved, he knew where to go.

My phone rang with a call from Ewan Garrett. "Just confirming we're on for Saturday," he said.

"Absolutely. Your folks will start arriving at 11:30, right? I'll be here at 11:00 to make sure we're ready for you. We're set up for you to use the picnic area and the kitchen. And if anyone wants a tour of the facilities I'm happy to accommodate. One thing, though. You guys are responsible for cleaning up. If there's any kind of mess I'll have to back-charge you."

"You don't have to worry about that. Some of our moms are fierce about cleaning."

"I'm just curious, and tell me if it's none of my business. What's the ratio of moms to dads?"

"I'd say we're about seventy-five percent moms, a mix of widows, divorcées, and parents by choice. Of the men, about half are gay, the other half usually widowed." He took a breath. "My wife died two years ago, leaving me with a four-year-old. The group has been a real lifesaver for me."

"I'm sorry to hear about your wife, but I'm glad the group has been helpful to you. I'm looking forward to giving you all a good time here at Friar Lake."

Ewan Garrett was young, only in his early thirties, and it must have been tragic to lose his wife so soon. I could only imagine how heart-rending it must have been, and then to have to soldier on for the sake of his child.

I pushed those thoughts away, because they came perilously close to reminding me of my own lost children, and went back to my Lalor research.

The earliest mention I found of Eckhardt Lalor in a business context was when he sold five hundred acres of land in Hamilton

Township to a real estate developer, who planned to build a housing development there. Shortly thereafter, Eckhardt was listed as the purchaser of four single-family homes on East State Street in Trenton. The article proudly proclaimed that Lalor, scion of a prominent local family, would be converting those homes into attractively priced apartments for lower income families.

And thus began Lalor's career as a slumlord. The date on the article was March 1955, some two years after Lalor returned from his military service in Korea. Doing some more cross-referencing, I found his father had died a few months earlier, most likely leaving him that undeveloped land.

Lalor was smart enough back then to realize he didn't have the resources to build new housing himself, so he liquidated that asset and reinvested it in ones that were more manageable.

Over the next few years, he accumulated property like dandruff on a collar. His early specialty was buying big houses in depressed areas of east and south Trenton and breaking them up into apartments. I remembered we often traveled up Prospect Street to get to our synagogue, and how those old brick houses with their broad porches had seemed so welcoming.

Looking at the map now, I saw that some of them had been converted, like the one Joey had worked on, while others had been torn down and replaced with square, featureless apartment buildings. From what I read, it seemed like Lalor took advantage of every government program to expand his operation, from low-income loans to subsidized rents for poor tenants.

He suffered some damage during the riots of 1967, following the assassination of Martin Luther King Jr. in April. He was quoted in the Trenton *Times* as defiantly stating he would rebuild affordable housing for indigent people, and not let a few bad apples ruin the lives of the innocent.

I caught a glimpse of myself in the window, and that reminded me Lili had suggested I get a haircut. I usually went to a chain operation at the Oxford Valley Mall, but I suddenly realized I had another option.

I went back to my research on Jennifer Zale. As I recalled, one of her clients was a hair salon called Connie's Curl Up and Dye. Mary had always confided everything in her stylist—she'd found out about the first miscarriage even before I did.

From Yelp, I discovered that Connie's was a one-woman salon, and that Connie got high marks from customers for her cheerful attitude. One called her a good listener, and another said she made haircuts fun with chatter and bad jokes.

Before I could second guess myself, I picked up the phone and called the salon. "I have a hair emergency," I said. "I'm taking my girlfriend out to dinner tonight, and she said that I've been looking shaggy. Any way you can fit me in this afternoon for a basic cut?"

"Well, I usually close at five, but business has been slow today, so if you can get here by four-forty-five I can squeeze you in."

"Awesome." I put the directions into my map and discovered if I left right away and paid only minor attention to posted speed signs, I could make it to the salon in time. Women were always bringing small yappy dogs into the place where I usually went, so I figured Rochester would be fine, especially if I was the last customer of the day.

Connie was surprised when we showed up. "You both look kind of shaggy," she said. "Which one of you am I supposed to cut?"

I raised my hand. "That would be me."

She waggled her clippers at Rochester, and he backed away at the buzzing sound. She laughed. "Guess that works, since your buddy doesn't like my technique."

Connie was a big woman with a low-cut blouse and lots of gold jewelry, and she reminded me of a lot of Italian women I'd known growing up, particularly some neighbors of my relatives in Chambersburg.

I settled down in the chair, and she said, "How'd you hear about me?"

"Yelp," I said, only stretching the truth a bit. "I grew up across the river and only moved to this side a few weeks ago, to move in with my girlfriend, so I've got to remake my Rolodex. You don't happen to know a good accountant, do you?"

That was all it took. "I could have referred you to a real sweetheart," she said. "But she took her own life a few months ago. Jumped right off the Calhoun Street Bridge."

As gray and brown hairs fell like autumn leaves onto the cape over my shirt, Connie told me, without ever mentioning Jennifer's name, all about her miscarriage, her layabout husband who had gone through four careers since their marriage, how she had trouble standing up to her demanding mother.

"She did the taxes for her family business," Connie said, hovering over my face so she could trim my errant eyebrows into shape. "Any time she found something suspicious her mother just pooh-poohed it and told her to ignore it. Jennifer told her mother that was going to come back and bite her some day. And then her mother goes and calls her a snake."

"Really? A snake?"

"Well, not exactly like that. Something about a snake biting her mother?"

"Could it be "How sharper than a serpent's tooth it is to have a thankless child?"

Connie stopped snipping and stepped back. "That's it! How do you know that?"

"It's Shakespeare. King Lear."

She looked dubious so I riffed, "I took Shakespeare at Pennsbury High. We had to put on that play for our final project."

She nodded. "Well, that was Jennifer and her mother. She brought Mom in here once, for a color, and I'll tell you, she never had a nice word to say about Jennifer. Her own daughter, can you believe that?"

Knowing how Anita's father had been with his kids, I could easily imagine that kind of behavior.

All the time my hair was getting cut, Rochester sprawled in front of a row of plastic chairs by the entrance. When Connie pulled the cape of me and stood up, that's when he did too. "Thanks for letting me bring the dog in," I said, as I pulled out my wallet.

"I'm a dog lover myself. I have a Malti-Poo at home. Loves to sleep next to my head and poke around in my bouffant."

"Fortunately, Rochester leaves my hair alone." I thanked Connie, gave her a big tip, and admired my haircut one more time in the mirror before heading home.

Over dinner, I told Lili what Connie had said about Jennifer's conflicts with her mother. "You think she found something wrong in the family business?"

"I don't know. But I wouldn't trust any of those Lalors as far as I could throw them."

After dinner, Lili said she needed cheering up, so we watched the remake of Doctor Dolittle starring Robert Downey Jr. I couldn't help noticing that he'd assembled a family of choice around him, who all loved and cared about each other regardless of species. Eckhardt Lalor had been the opposite, ruling his human family meanly. I remembered he'd complained whenever the kids when to the monkey house at the zoo.

Yeah, a Dolittle he wasn't.

Chapter 19
Bent

The next day was Friday the 13th. I guess you'd say I'm a superstitious person—I won't walk under ladders, I avoid black cats, and I tried to be very careful that day, because who knows what kind of bad mojo is out there, after all?

That morning, as I walked Rochester, I looked around at River Bend. When I was a kid, it was all part of a big farm, but because the water table was high near the river the fields were usually left fallow—the commercial machines used to plant and harvest by then would get stuck in the muck and break down.

It was only when I was living in California that I began to hear about a development there, from my father. An out-of-state builder had bought the farm property and begun a program to dredge the muck and use that to build up the surrounding land. They created a series of lakes, and platted waterfront properties around them.

By then, my mother had passed away and my father was looking for a smaller, more manageable house. "I've been out to see this new community on the north edge of town," I remember he told me. "They call it River Bend. They've put a lot of money into draining and reformatting the land."

That was my father, ever the engineer. "They're taking measurements of the water table all over and they're putting in a special drainage system to make sure the neighborhood doesn't flood."

I admit I wasn't paying much attention, though every weekend when I spoke to him he had something more to say about River Bend. "They finally have townhouse models up," he said one day. "I bought one."

"You what?"

"I've been talking about the damned townhouse for a month or more, Steven," my father said. "Haven't you been paying attention?"

"I thought it was just conversation. Don't you want to retire to Florida like Aunt Edna and Uncle Bert?"

"My sister hates the cold, and my brother-in-law doesn't like to shovel snow. Me, I like a change of seasons, and at River Bend they'll have gardeners to take away the snow and the falling leaves. I won't have to worry about anything."

"But a townhouse? What about the stairs?"

"I'm still quite capable of climbing a flight of stairs. Do me good to get some exercise in the house."

After that I gave up. Mary was pregnant, and then my dad was sick, and I simply accepted the townhouse when my father passed. I moved in and had never looked into any of the infrastructure, trusting my dad knew what he was talking about.

But after hearing so much about Lalor's business I was curious to see who had been behind River Bend, and if everyone in the neighborhood had been as happy as my father.

When Rochester and I returned from our walk, I sat down at the kitchen table with my laptop and did the kind of research I should have done before I moved into the place.

Once again, I had to rely on access to the Eastern library to get the old articles from the *Courier-Times*. There had been an uproar when the plans for the farmland were announced, mostly NIMBYs.

I had learned in a job long before that NIMBY stood for "Not in my backyard." People who recognized the need for a new shopping center or residential development, perhaps, though didn't want it

Dog's Waiting Room

right where they lived. There had been complaints about construction traffic going down Main Street, disruption of wildlife in the preserve, and so on.

Eventually the complaints continued, and the developer backed out, after the land had already been dredged and platted. The company sold out to a local operation called River Bend LLC, who managed the construction and then sale of the mix of single-family homes and townhouses.

From then on, the publicity had been much better. Local builders, it was speculated, were more in tune with what Stewart's Crossing residents wanted. There was a fancy ribbon-cutting ceremony.

By the time I moved in, two years after construction, the oaks and maples were getting tall enough to provide a shady canopy in the summer. The management company hired landscapers to keep the grass cut and the hedges trimmed. It wasn't new, but it was new-ish.

Lately I'd been hearing about construction problems from neighbors. The shower pan in some second-floor bathrooms wasn't installed correctly, causing leaks to the dining-room ceiling. The bathrooms weren't perfectly sealed, and bugs could crawl in. Lili had discovered a fairly large spider nest between the vanity and the wall in the guest bathroom, which resulted in a scream in Spanish that chilled me to the bone.

I did a quick search on River Bend, LLC, and an involuntary, "Oh, no," escaped my mouth and caused Rochester to look up.

The principals for that LLC were Eckhardt and Jeffrey Lalor.

Some further searching found another LLC called Mercer Greens under the same ownership, and which had constructed a small neighborhood by that name in Ewing Township. The pattern had been the same – an out of down developer had come into an underdeveloped area, done the grading work to smooth out some hillsides and dam a small creek, forming lakes.

Then they had run into trouble with permitting and community outrage, and sold off to Mercer Greens LLC, which had completed the buildout. I didn't know what I expected to find, but I wanted to take a look at it. I bundled Rochester into the car and off we went.

We crossed the river at Washington's Crossing and then headed south. Route 29 there was still quite rural, with only the occasional hardware store or takeout restaurant. The road paralleled the Delaware and Raritan Canal, the one on the Jersey side, and I remembered my mother telling me that the stone walls alongside the road had been built by the WPA back in the Depression.

Two curving stone walls announced the entrance to Mercer Greens, like they did at River Bend, but there the similarity stopped. The landscaping was more barren, and I could only see townhouses, no larger single-family properties.

From what I understood, the original developers had come up with the house exteriors and floor plans in River Bend, and platted out the streets. Hence the quirk that many of my neighbors' homes looked like they could have been transported from Russia, with brick towers and multi-paned windows, and lots of gray copper details. Our streets were also named for cities in the Pale of Settlement, the western region of Russia.

These were more generic buildings, like many cheap structures scattered around Bucks and Mercer counties. Interrupted pediments over the doors, bland brick walls, and flat metal roofs with downspouts.

I saw an older man weeding a flower bed and parked nearby, then put Rochester on his leash for a walk. The man saw us approach and sat up to watch us. "Morning," I said.

He glared at me. Cut to the chase.

I glanced around and was happy to see a couple of for sale signs. "I'm thinking of buying a property here," I said. "Wanted to come take a look at the neighborhood without the real estate agent breathing down my neck."

"Wouldn't, if I were you," the man said. "Wish I'd never."

"Really? What's wrong?"

"Builder skimped on everything. Already had to replace my air conditioning compressor with a larger unit—the one they put in didn't cool the upstairs. New washer dryer, dishwasher, refrigerator, you name it."

"How long have you been here?"

"Five years," he said.

Beside me, Rochester was sniffing the lawn. "Don't you let that dog pee on my grass," the man said, and I jerked Rochester's leash.

"Sorry."

We went back to the car, though I let him pee once where I didn't see anyone looking.

I had gathered all the information I needed by then. Eckhardt Lalor was a hard man, mean to his family and cheap when it came to the living accommodations of others. I wondered how many of the problems I'd had with my townhouse could be traced back to his shoddy practices.

When I got home, Lili was there, having shut down the Art History department early on Friday afternoon. "Been going through all this paperwork Fedi sent me," she said.

I sat beside her at the dining room table and looked at the neat piles. Each one seemed to represent a different asset. "Sometimes I wish my mother hadn't been so equal," she said. "Instead of saying divide everything after her death, she could have left a couple of the accounts to me and a couple to Fedi."

I shrugged. "She probably didn't think of it that way. And what if one account had done much better than another, and Fedi got the big one. Or you did?"

"I think we'd make it up to each other. This way is much more confusing."

"Rick showed me Lalor's will," I said.

She looked at me. "Really? As opposed to you finding it?"

"Wills are public documents. I think he just gave it to me for background, because there weren't any big surprises. Except for a collection of his first wife's Lenox pieces he wanted given to the Trenton Historical Society."

"I'll bet you wanted to see those," she said. "Or your mother would have."

I shrugged. "I've seen a lot of that old Lenox. Most of it's not my taste."

Rochester came over and rested his head on my leg, to remind me that he existed, and he deserved attention just as much as Eckhardt Lalor did.

I ran my hand down his back, releasing a hailstorm of golden fluff. "Someone needs to be furminated," I said. I loved the tool by that name, which scratched deep through his layers of fur to pull out dead hair.

I fetched the tool and a plastic grocery bag, and sat on the tile floor in the living room. In long, slow strokes with the toothed comb, I pulled off piles of hair. Some of it got away from me and went floating through the air like golden angel wings.

When Lili came downstairs, my black shorts were covered in fur, and there were piles of golden strands around us on the floor. "I'll get the vacuum," she said.

"Wait a minute." I stood up and began to wiggle like a 70s disco wannabe. "Shake shake shake," I chanted. "Shake your puppy!"

Rochester got the clue, and gave his body a massive shake, releasing even more hair into the air. "Now you can vacuum." I picked up the grocery bag full of hair. "We've almost got enough hair for a new puppy."

"God forbid," Lili said.

I moved the furniture and she vacuumed, and Rochester went upstairs to get away from the noise—and spread the hairy love up there.

While she was cleaning, I picked up a few petals that had drifted off Adriano's arrangement. Certain flowers had begun to droop, like in a Baroque painting, and I admired the look while calculating how many more days before we'd have to toss it.

After she put the vacuum away, Lili came to join me on the sofa. "We lived in a pretty lousy place when we first came to the US," she said. "What I'd call slums today. We had a one-bedroom apartment in a run-down building where Fedi and I switched between the couch and a sleeping bag on the floor every night. Where my mother had to fight with the gas to get the stove to light, where there was never enough hot water for all of us in the bathroom. But I was a little kid then, so those things didn't matter much to me."

"But for your family, Kansas City was a bump on the road," I said. "Your father was educated and he kept getting better jobs."

"He was also Jewish and his first language was Spanish. It couldn't have been easy for him." She leaned against the back of the sofa and put her legs up on the coffee table. "The Jewish aid agencies helped us at first. They're the ones who got us the apartment in Kansas City. But after that my mother said no—she would pick her own place to live. And I know, she was fortunate to be able to do that."

I shifted position so that I was turned sideways on the couch, looking at her.

"In Buffalo Grove we lived in an apartment on the first floor of a townhouse. When we moved to Long Island, my parents were able to buy our first house. It was small and on a busy street, but it was ours."

"And then?"

"Then I left for college. They stayed in New York until Fedi finished high school and then they were on the move again. My father got his final job, with a government contractor in Arlington, Virginia, and they traded up again. A split-level house, with a front and back yard and an in-ground swimming pool. It was too big for just the two of them, but it was their American dream."

"Kind of like Jeffrey Lalor's house in Crossing Estates. Way too big for him and his son. But knowing the kind of housing his father owned in Trenton I'm sure he was making a statement."

"People use real estate for all kinds of funny purposes," Lili said. "Back when I was taking pictures full-time I was often sent out on assignment for home and décor magazines. I got this sense of who lived there from my photos. Immigrants who'd made it big used a lot of gold paint and big white carpets, like they could afford to have parts of the house where nobody actually lived. Collectors were more focused on how and where to hang their art than on comfort or convenience. Some houses were all about the view, as if the inside didn't matter."

"I'll bet a decorator put together Jeffrey Lalor's house. I had this feeling a stranger bought the artwork and the furniture and arranged it to look like a family lived there."

"That's one sad family," Lili said.

"After Mr. Lalor's funeral I had this urge to go see the cemetery where my parents and grandparents are. At least my mother's parents. I don't actually know where my father's parents are—I think somewhere in North Jersey."

She pulled her legs back and curled them under her, and turned to face me. "I went to Havana for a job once, God, decades ago. I found the Jewish cemetery, all overgrown. I spent a whole afternoon there, clearing out weeds and planting new flowers. And then I took a ton of pictures and sent them to my mother."

"And?"

"And she had nothing more to say than 'That's nice, *mamita*.' She had already put them behind when she left Cuba." She looked at me. "Did I tell you she had my father cremated?"

"Isn't he buried beside her, in Miami?"

"He was, eventually. But when he died, she knew she wasn't staying in Arlington, so she wasn't going to bury him there. She bought an urn and carried his ashes with her to Miami. It wasn't until she was settled there and decided that was her last stop that she had the ashes buried in a plot."

"Lalor's first two wives are on either side of him," I said. "Did your parents always sleep on the same side of the bed?"

"Of course. Didn't yours?"

"Oh, yeah. And when my mother died, my father had her put in the plot on the right. So that they would be sleeping beside each other for eternity the way they had in life."

Lil's eyes opened wide. "I didn't realize that. It's the same way with my parents."

I reached for her hand. "Together forever," I said. "It's kind of grim, but at the same time I like it."

She took my hand in hers, her slim fingers wrapped around mine. "Me, too."

Chapter 20
Slumlord

I usually take the River Road a few miles above speed limit (well, more than a few, but I wouldn't tell Rick that) but Saturday morning I drove as sedately as if I was in a hearse. It must have been all the death around me, but I wanted to make sure I enjoyed living, before I couldn't anymore.

It's surprising the things you spot when you're going slowly – a flattened squirrel in the middle of an intersection, piles of weeds tossed out by farmers. But at the same time patches of black-eyed Susans, the glint of ripe blackberries in a hedge.

The good and the bad.

I made it up the hill to Friar Lake without incident, and took Rochester for a quick walk. I was too edgy to let him go off leash, though.

While waiting for Ewan Garrett's group, I answered a few emails and signed a couple of online invoices. Then I went back to my research on Lalor Properties.

As the 1960s turned into the 70s and 80s, there were more complaints about Lalor's management company. Deferred maintenance led to infestations of rats and roaches. Broken plumbing was slow to be fixed, and damaged roofs even slower to be repaired.

Eckhardt Lalor was rarely quoted in those stories. The tag line seemed to be "A spokesman for Lalor Properties declined to comment."

One of his common opponents was Solomon Jackson, whose park I had visited the other day. He often stood against Lalor in disputes with landlords, medical groups and city departments. He would have been a great suspect in Lalor's death, if he himself hadn't died the year before.

He had been eulogized throughout the state and region as a visionary in social justice. I was surprised to see Eckhardt Lalor mentioned in an article Jackson's son Moses had written shortly after his father's death. "My father worked hard on behalf of his fellow man, often compromising his own health to do so," he wrote. He listed Eckhardt Lalor as one of his father's chief combatants, one of several men whose venality and obstinacy had driven his father to an early grave.

Did that give Moses Jackson a motive to kill Lalor? Resentment is a powerful emotion. I did some quick research on Moses.

Instead of following his father into social action, Moses had chosen the ministry. He led the Mount Tabor AME Zion Baptist Church in Trenton. His name was often listed as a co-claimant in lawsuits his father brought against Lalor.

Many of the suits had been dismissed after Lalor made repairs to buildings, or after Lalor's company sold the properties to someone else. Lalor had only countersued once, claiming that by constantly referring to him as a slumlord, Solomon and Moses Jackson had damaged his personal reputation and his ability to conduct business.

Lalor had mobilized many of his colleagues from those charitable groups like the Lions and the Elks to testify on his behalf, and Lalor won a million-dollar claim against both Jacksons. Neither had liability insurance, and Solomon had been forced to sell his family home, and Moses's salary at the church had been garnished.

Solomon had died a few years later, and Moses agreed to make no further claims against Lalor in exchange for a cancellation of the amount still owed.

Did Moses hold a grudge against Eckhardt Lalor? How about a kid who'd grown up in one of his slum properties? Children raised in decaying homes were vulnerable to all sorts of ailments. Perhaps an adult today blamed a congenital health issue on growing up in a Lalor property?

That seemed far-fetched, even to me.

I was about to push the Jacksons aside when I discovered that Moses had a daughter, Annie, who was twenty-two, and she worked through an agency as a home health aide. I found her name on the agency's website where she was listed as not only "caring," but also "strong, able to lift and transport heavy patients."

Was it possible that she had cared for Eckhardt Lalor at some point? Did she carry a resentment against him for what had been done to her father and grandfather?

And did she have an alibi for the day Lalor died?

I didn't have time to do any more searching, though, because a timer on my phone rang to alert me that the Parents without Partners would be arriving soon, and I wanted to be ready for them.

Chapter 21
Parents

Ewan was the first to arrive, with a banner he asked me to help him put up, welcoming the group. His son Gawain was a six-year-old handful, and it took all Rochester's energy to keep the boy under control while his father and I worked.

Unlike his father, Gawain was blond, and sturdily built. "He's all boy, aren't you, kid," he said, as he picked the boy up. "Trains, cars, running, jumping. Thank God there will be other kids here to wear him out."

Cars and SUVs began arriving up the long hilly road that led to Friar Lake. Gawain quickly recognized a friend, and took off with the other boy and his mom while Ewan and I shared host duties.

After a while I left him there and went down to check on the kitchen and picnic areas. These parents had their act together—a couple of moms in the kitchen, the rest out by the picnic area. A pair of dads were putting up soccer goals while other parents were unpacking food or supervising the kids.

I helped out where necessary, but most of the time I stood at the edge of a field and watched. It was fascinating to imagine what circumstances had led all these people together—the joy of births or adoptions, the pain of divorce or death. I watched Ewan and Gawain play soccer, and marveled at my colleague's ability to keep running after his son whenever he strayed toward the woods. Ewan was perhaps a dozen years younger than I was—had I had that much energy back then?

Or was I crouched over my laptop, avoiding my wife and any thoughts about kids?

When Ewan gave up playing soccer and sent Gawain off with a couple of moms and kids, he came to join me at the edge of the field. "I need a drink," he said, wiping the sweat from his brow. "Want something?"

"I guess." I followed him along the edge of the field to a haphazard pile of coolers.

"Nothing alcoholic, I'm afraid," he said, as he searched through half-melted ice. "We don't want the kids to accidentally get hold of something. Lemonade, budget cola, or iced tea."

"Lemonade, please," I said, and he handed me a bottle of what I considered lemonade-flavored drink, the kind where most of the ingredients had long chemical names. But I was hot and it was cold.

"How often do you guys get together?" I asked.

"We have a couple of events a month. Usually focused around the kids—we go to museums in small groups, outdoor festivals, concerts. Every once in a while we'll organize a massive babysitting session so that some of the parents can get together without kids around. And the internet makes things so much easier—anytime I have a question or a problem with Gawain, I can log on and get answers." He smiled. "Sometimes too many answers."

He took a swig of his lemonade. "I'm grateful every day that I have Gawain. His mom and I weren't actually married, though I tell most people we were, to simplify things. When she died, neither of us had wills, and her parents tried to take Gawain away from me."

"Wow."

"I admit, I fell apart for a while. Harper was my everything, and when she died I went on a massive binge. School was out and I wasn't teaching during the summer—supposed to be working on a book, you know. Instead I drank a lot, held onto Gawain and cried. Her parents swooped in, said I wasn't competent, and hired an attorney."

He took another swig of lemonade. "That's when I realized it was real, that Harper was gone and she wasn't coming back, and that she'd want me to shape up and look after Gawain. It was embarrassing—I had to pee in a cup every week for six months to ensure I wasn't using anything. Her parents said some terrible things, and I kept reminding myself that I couldn't lash out at them because they'd lost their daughter."

He smiled. "The moral of the story is that everybody needs a will. If Harper had put her wishes in writing as soon as Gawain was born, I would have had a lot less trouble."

Most of the parents at Friar Lake that day were white, though some of the kids had color in their background. I thought about all the single-parent families that struggled in Eckhardt Lalor's properties, how much they might have enjoyed being out in the country like this, and how much their moms and dads might have appreciated the chance to share their burdens with others.

I couldn't help contrasting them to Eckhardt Lalor's kids and grandkids. They were white children of privilege, and even if the Nitzes had been forced to go to public school instead of private, they'd had multiple advantages simply by their skin color, and what their families expected of them.

What about Noah Lalor, though? If his father was broke and his mother wouldn't pay his tuition, he wouldn't be able to continue at Harvey Mudd. Would he transfer to a cheaper school? Drop out in anger and rebellion? I knew adults who had dreamed of expensive educations that their parents couldn't or wouldn't pay for, and how that resentment had dogged their lives.

Was it enough to cause him to push his grandfather into the Delaware, though?

Late that afternoon, the Parents Without Partners began to clean up, and by the time they left it was as if they'd never been. Good for them, and good for me, because I didn't have to do anything more than stack the trash cans to be emptied on Monday, and I didn't have to write up an invoice for Ewan's group.

We drove home, and Rochester was so worn out by playing with all the kids that he didn't even want to go out for a quick pee. Instead he flopped on the sofa and went right to sleep.

When Rochester heard Lili's car in the driveway, he jumped up, barking a welcome to her. I went into the kitchen to see what I could make for dinner, and I was fishing around in the freezer when Lili came in.

"Can we go out tonight?" she asked. "It's been a long week and I feel like being spoiled."

I closed the freezer door. "Happy to spoil you," I said, and we kissed hello. Then I leaned back against the counter. "Any ideas?"

She shrugged. "How about you?"

I remembered the lottery gift card for Fiddler's Creek Lodge that Rochester had found. I pulled it out of my wallet and showed it to Lili. "Ever heard of this place?"

"Oh, Gracious Chigwe told me about it. She said it has an outdoor terrace overlooking the Delaware. She and her husband like it because they can take their bichon with them." She grabbed her phone and typed. "Let's see what their menu is like."

She hummed for a moment, then said, "Generic steakhouse, which is fine with me. Oh, and look, they have a rating of four dog bones for canine service."

"How can we resist a four-bone review?" I looked over at Rochester. "How about you, puppy? But don't think you're getting four bones out of this dinner. You'll be lucky with one."

He ambled over to me and nuzzled my hand. "That's his vote."

We were in the car a short time later, with Rochester in the back seat, when Lili said, "Remember we were looking for my mother's ring when we were in Florida? I forgot to ask Fedi about it when we were there, and he called me today to ask if I'd taken it."

"I'm assuming you didn't."

"No. I did go through her jewelry box, and I took a couple of pieces. A gold pinkie ring her mother gave her, that she always wore. A turquoise and silver necklace my father bought her when we went to Hoover Dam. And a bunch of silver hair clips. They wouldn't look good on Sara's blonde hair."

"Did you see the ring when you went through the box?"

She shook her head. "I assumed Fedi had already taken it."

"Who else had access to the box?"

We reached Scudder Falls Bridge and I crossed the river. The steakhouse was a couple of miles upriver, just above us, on a bluff overlooking the Delaware.

"I've been thinking about that," Lili said. "He already asked Sara. And I don't think that either Bella or Rafi know enough or care enough about jewelry. Then I remembered that my mother tore a tendon in her arm about a year ago, and Fedi insisted that she have an aide for a few weeks to help her."

"I thought she hated that idea."

"She did. The agency sent a different person each day and by the end of the week she said *No mas*."

"I suppose you or Fedi could call the agency and see if they can trace which aides were in her house when. Then see if any of them had complaints for theft."

"I suggested that. But Fedi surprised me."

I pulled into the parking lot. The restaurant was busy, but I spotted a few tables at the outside terrace that overlooked the river. "How?"

"He said neither of us wanted the ring for sentimental reasons, and neither of us need the money we would have gotten for selling it."

"So?"

"He said those aides get paid so little to do the work that we won't do for our families. He wasn't going to accuse someone and maybe have her lose her job."

"But it's theft."

I got out, and then opened the back door for Rochester, grabbing his leash as he jumped out.

Lili came around to my side of the car and threaded her arm through mine. "I know. I told him, what if next time this person steals from someone who can't afford the loss? Or takes something very meaningful."

After my ill-advised computer break-in at the three major credit bureaus, the judge had looked down at me over the rims of her eyeglasses. "Most of the other offenders in this court are teenagers who don't know any better," she had said. "You're a grown man with two college degrees. What possessed you to not only commit this crime, but think you could get away with it?"

I remember staring at her with my mouth open for a moment. My attorney had already stated the circumstances of the case—I had hacked in so that I could keep my wife from running up our credit card bills in the wake of her second miscarriage.

Finally I said, "I'm sorry, your honor. After losing that baby, my heart broke, and my brain shut down. That's all I can say."

"I've seen many, many cases where a predatory credit agency has ruined someone's life, so I'm tempted to lean on your behalf and call this a victimless crime. You didn't steal anything, and you've cooperated with the bureaus involved to demonstrate how you were able to get in. You've even shown them what they can do to keep others out. But you committed a crime, nonetheless, and the state requires punishment."

She had sent me to a minimum-security facility in San Bernardino County, where most of the men I met were non-violent offenders. Cat burglars, white collar criminals, and so on. Because I had a background as an English teacher, I worked with inmates who needed to create resumes or write cover letters for jobs. Many of those I spoke to had stolen out of need—to feed their families, pay their electric bills, and so on.

A few, though, including all the white-collar men, had no economic reason for committing their crimes. Like me, they had done what they had done for emotional reasons—to get revenge on an employer who'd done them wrong, or because they wanted a bigger house or fancier car or private jet to calm some interior need.

Lili, Rochester and I walked up to the podium in front of the door, and the hostess led us around to the terrace. Our server was Dustin, a young college kid in a hunter green vest with a fiddle embroidered on it, and we both ordered cocktails with a bowl of water for Rochester. It was a lovely evening, the sky darkening to a vibrant purple. Down below us we saw the river moving lazily downstream.

Dustin came back and recited the specials. Lili ordered the teriyaki chicken, a perennial favorite of hers, and I got the prime rib. "And our hairy friend will have the doggie beef loaf," I said. "How is that prepared?"

"Ground beef rolled with celery, carrots, diced apple, eggs, white bread, and rolled oats. Baked in tomato sauce in miniature loaf pans."

Lili agreed that sounded like something Rochester would like. When Dustin was gone I looked at Lili. "We don't know who stole your mother's ring or why. I'm afraid I have to agree with Fedi not to pursue it. I believe in karmic justice—those who do good in the world are rewarded, and those who do evil are punished, even if that punishment only happens inside them."

"Did you believe that before you went to prison?"

"Nope. If I had, I doubt I'd have ended up in prison at all. And then I probably wouldn't have come back to Stewart's Crossing and I wouldn't have met you. I did the crime, I did the time, and I've moved on."

"And I'm glad you did," she said.

When Lili went to the restroom to wash her hands, I ran through our conversation, because something about it had ticked a box in my head.

I went backwards, to the question of Senorita Weinstock's aides. That triggered what I had learned about the youngest Jackson,

Annie, the home health aide. How could I check to see if she had ever worked for the Lalors?

She had grown up around her grandfather's anger toward Eckhardt Lalor, and seen how the lawsuit had ruined her family. At twenty-two, she was old enough to seek vengeance. I pulled out my phone and sent a text to Rick, asking him to get a list of the aides who had taken care of Lalor in the past, and if any of them had felt slighted by the old man.

Lili came back as I was finishing. "Connecting with an old prison buddy?" she asked with a smile as she slid back into the wooden booth.

"Rick. And the only prison we have in common is matrimony."

She laughed. "Do you really feel that way?"

"Well, let's see. Marriage is an institution, and when you enter into it you promise to stay for life." I held up my hands as if I was balancing. "Life in an institution, life in prison."

She laughed. "Remind me of that if we ever think about getting married."

Chapter 22
Wives

Dustin brought our salads, and we dug in. Lili and I had talked, off and on, about getting married, but so far we'd been happy as we were, and neither of us felt obliged to change.

The wind shifted and I sniffed the air, smelling the scent of tobacco, and looked around. None of the other diners were smoking, though it was still legal to smoke outdoors at restaurants. At my feet, Rochester rolled on his side and put his right paw up against his nose, as if he was trying to block the smell of the smoke. His nose was a lot more sensitive than a human's so it wasn't surprising that he didn't like it.

I noticed a woman in the same green vest as Dustin leaning against the back wall of the restaurant, smoking a cigarette. As she dropped the butt to the pavement and ground it out, an Asian man in a suit came outside.

"Genevieve, I told you not to smoke out here. The smell goes over to the customers and they complain."

She looked toward the patio and yelled, "Somebody over there complain about a hard-working woman who needs a break now and then? Well, fuck you all!"

"Jenny." He took her arm.

"Get your fucking hand off me." Then she stalked back into the restaurant.

"Well, that's this evening's entertainment," I said.

"Poor thing. She's not having a good day. I was a server once, for about three days when I was in college, and I couldn't take it."

A few minutes later, the man in the suit was back, walking around the patio talking to customers. "Sorry for the disturbance," he said, when he came to us. "Jenny's not well, and sometimes the pain gets to her. I hope you won't let her outburst ruin your dinner, and that you'll come back and see us again soon."

He handed Lili his business card, on which he'd written, "Have a drink on me," with his initials. We hadn't ordered drinks, but I had noticed the restaurant had some specialty cocktails at fifteen dollars.

"Wow." I looked around the patio. "There are ten tables out here. That's a hundred fifty bucks. An expensive apology."

"But it's not money out of his pocket until we come back, and when we do, we'll certainly order dinner again."

Our food was fine, and Rochester gobbled his doggie beef loaf eagerly. I did feel sorry for Jenny, though. I understood what it was like to reach the end of your rope.

We spent a slow and relaxed Sunday, and when Lili went upstairs for a nap I went back to my research on the Lalors. I didn't see Jeffrey Lalor mentioned online until 1995, when he was identified as a vice-president of the company and he had engineered the sale of a dozen properties in South Trenton, near the prison, to a company that planned to demolish them and build a large nursing home on the land.

Gradually the references to Eckhardt Lalor trailed off. He was no longer attending meetings or contributing to social service organizations.

Whenever I found an actual street address, I went back to the

Property Appraiser's Office and tracked its history. It seemed that Lalor Properties continued to sell off its inventory, in ones and twos.

There was a transfer of several apartment buildings to a company called JAP Investments in 2005. For a few minutes I assumed it was a Japanese company, and then put together the initials for Jeffrey, Anita and Peter.

At that point, according to official records, Lalor Properties ceased to exist. Eckhardt Lalor was the president of JAP, with Jeffrey as vice president and Anita and Peter as members of the board.

Records were vague, but it appeared that JAP had income in excess of one million dollars a year, but under ten million. It had broadened its scope, and moved to the suburbs, purchasing small shopping centers and apartment buildings in Mercer and Bucks counties.

Lalor had remained in the big house on the edge of Cadwalader Park until 2002. When he sold the house, he moved to a two-bedroom luxury condominium apartment in Yardley, right along the Delaware River. That property, owned by JAP, had then been sold a few years later.

Was that when Lalor's memory started to go, and he had moved in with Jeffrey and his family? Soon after that, Vivian Lalor had been hired by a Silicon Valley startup. If Eckhardt was half as cranky as people said, it must have been a relief for her to get out of that house after he joined them.

Chapter 23
Cascade

That evening Lili and I were having dinner when she said, "I spoke to Fedi this afternoon. Sara was cleaning up in Rafi's room and found my mother's diamond ring."

"Really? What did Rafi want with it?"

"He said that his grandmother always intended him to have it for his bride. So he took it."

"Bride? How old is this kid anyway?"

"Almost fourteen. But he's planning for the future."

We both laughed. "What do Fedi and Sara say?"

"That the best place for the ring is in their safe deposit box. Actually I think Sara wanted that stone for a pendant but she can't compete with her son."

She sat back. "I realized that I've been talking to Fedi a lot more over the last couple of weeks than during the last few years."

"Is that good or bad?"

"A mix. Sometimes we'll be in the middle of an argument, and one of us will dig up an old grudge or a sweet memory, and we'll laugh like we did when we were kids." She used her napkin, then put it down. "I know it's self-evident, but I realized that he's my brother, *mi hermano*, and I love him. I don't want to lose this connection we have, now that my mother's not around to be the nexus. He and I both have to reach out and figure new ways of keeping in touch."

Then the roof fell down.

I was sitting at the kitchen table, facing Lili, and behind her the patio. At the loud groaning noise, I looked up in alarm. "What's the..." I began, as I watched the valance over the sliding glass doors come loose from the wall in a slow motion that a movie maker would have been proud of.

Lili had been sitting with her back to the patio, and she jumped up as the tangle of green fabric slats and metal chains cascaded to the floor. The noise scared the heck out of Rochester, and it made my pulse race as I pushed back from the table and stood up.

When my father moved into the townhouse, he had a decorator help him fix it up, and she had chosen floor-to-ceiling vertical blinds to shade the sliding glass doors that faced west. They were hung from long horizontal valances that were fastened to the wall above the doors.

Once we were all recovered, Rochester began snooping through the pile of fabric and metal and Lili had to pull him away to avoid him cutting himself on anything.

I stood up on a kitchen chair and surveyed the damage. The drywall above the doors felt damp. Why? What had caused the cascade of blinds?

Our kitchen sits beneath a spare bedroom which Lili used as her in-home office. There's a sliding door there, out to a small Juliet balcony. The grout had come loose there a year or so before, and I'd had someone come in and repair it. But it looked like rainwater had gotten into the drywall and weakened it, leading to the eventual collapse.

Great. Another excellent construction by Lalor Properties.

Lili and I worked together to undo all the blinds and fold them up for recycling. "It was time we redecorated anyway," I said, as I pulled the remaining nails loose. "You want to look online for something you like?"

We got in bed and tried to share a laptop to look for blinds, but Rochester had been shaken by the incident and he clambered between us. We ended up mirroring my iPad to the TV and watching YouTube videos until bedtime.

Because I'd worked on Saturday, and knew I had little to keep me busy at Friar Lake, on Monday morning I decided to take Rochester out for a special walk, back along the river. I don't know what kept me going back to that area, except that it represented an unsolved mystery that my brain continued to pull at the threads of.

We parked at our usual lay-by and I kept Rochester on his leash while I looked around. We hadn't been there for more than two or three minutes when a huge Akita came running through the undergrowth towards us, growling menacingly.

Before I could react, he had Rochester's throat in his jaws. I tried kicking the dog, with no result, until I remembered that if you cut off the dog's air supply, he'll have to open his mouth to breathe.

I knelt down and stuck my hand under the Akita's chain collar and began to twist. Out of the corner of my ear I heard someone yell, "Sumo! Sumo!" and then a young man burst out into the clearing.

I was pulling and twisting with all my might. "What are you doing to my dog!" the young man cried.

"Trying to get him off mine!"

Rochester was strangely quiet, as if his brain was processing this strange form of play that must have been painful. Seconds ticked away as I struggled to cut off the Akita's airway. I finally managed to get enough traction that the dog's jaws opened, and Rochester scrambled back. "This dog is vicious!" I said. "You need to keep him on a leash."

Still grasping the Akita's collar, I transferred ownership to the boy, who hooked on his leash. Looking closely, I realized that I recognized him. "You're Noah Lalor," I said. I backed away, holding onto Rochester's leash. "Your father is going to hear about this."

"No! You can't tell him. He'll take Sumo away."

"And have him put down," I said. "There's no room in this world for vicious dogs." I clutched Rochester's leash in my hands. "Your whole family is brutal. Somebody probably pushed your grandfather into the water and drowned him. Did you do that? Because you wanted your inheritance?"

His mouth gaped open.

"Twenty-five thousand bucks," I said. "Must seem like a lot of money to a kid like you. Then again, wouldn't go far toward tuition at Harvey Mudd."

"How do you know that?"

"I know a lot of things," I said. "Your grandfather was a slumlord and your father's a business failure. Bad genes run your family."

I got Rochester into the car and locked the doors. Then I looked at his face. There were a couple of puncture marks on his jaw and throat but only a little blood.

I was probably more shaken than he was. I rested my head against his golden one and cried for a moment, and he tried to lick my face.

As soon as I had my composure, I turned the car on and drove directly to our vet, Dr. Horz. Rochester was reluctant to get out of the car, and I had to lean down and comfort him for a moment or two. "It's all right, boy. I'm sorry that nasty dog hurt you, but we'll get you all patched up."

Finally he was willing to jump out, and we walked into the vet's office, where the receptionist hustled us quickly into an exam room. Dr. Horz, a small, slim woman with prematurely gray hair, came in moments later. "What's wrong with our beautiful boy?" she asked.

I pointed to his snout and explained about the Akita attack. "Good thing you were right there to pull him off," she said. "Do you know the owner?"

"I do. I'm going to report him to the police as soon as I know how badly Rochester is hurt."

"You'll want to make sure the dog has his rabies shots," she said. "Although I doubt that will be a problem. These are only surface wounds and we'll be able to treat them with some local antibiotics."

She patched him up quickly. "Does he eat solid or liquid food?"

"Kibble."

"Good. You don't want food to get into these cuts. Just keep them clean and apply this ointment twice a day, and he'll be fine." She leaned her head down to his. "Yes, you will, won't you, you handsome boy."

Despite what was supposed to be a slow, easy summer, I had a cascade of problems. Eckhardt Lalor's murder, Lili's mother's death, and now the harm done to my dog.

On my way home, I called Rick and told him what had happened. "I'll send you a form to fill out," he said. "There's a fine for unleashed dogs in Stewart's Crossing, and under state law Lalor will be responsible for your veterinary bill."

"I want to call and yell at him."

"I'd rather you didn't, honestly. You're already caught up in this investigation of his father's death, and you getting in his face about his son's dog will only complicate matters."

"But I'm angry!"

"I know. I'd be lethal if anything happened to Rascal. But I'd appreciate it if you could fill out the paperwork and leave it at that. I don't want to hear about officers being called out to mediate an argument between you two."

"I wasn't going to get in his face," I grumbled. "But I did say some things to Noah."

"Things? What kind of things?"

I felt ashamed that I'd taken out my wrath over the dog bite, and my frustration over not knowing what happened to Eckhardt Lalor, on a teenager. "I might have suggested he pushed his grandfather into the water and drowned him."

"You did not. Really?"

"And I said a few choice words about his father and his grandfather."

"Well, that certainly stirs the pot. But you can't say anything more. Promise me."

I looked over at Rochester, and because he was on his side I couldn't see the puncture wounds. All I saw was my sweet dog. I reached out and stroked his flank.

"I'll do my best to stay calm," I said. "Rochester will help with that."

The big golden looked up at me and grinned, even after all he'd been through that day. If he could manage to overcome fear and anger, so could I.

"Did you find out anything new about Lalor?" I asked.

"Nothing dramatic. I spoke to the accountant who took over the tax paperwork from Jennifer Zale. He thought everything was in fine shape, though Anita was worried Jennifer had screwed something up that might have led to her suicide."

"But the company wasn't hiding anything?"

"Not as far as this guy told me. Yeah, they might have accelerated depreciation on some of the properties, but nothing against the law."

"No motive for suicide or Lalor's murder, then?"

"Sorry to disappoint you. This accountant knew Jennifer Zale well, went to college with her, the couples were good friends. He puts all the blame for her suicide on post-partum depression."

I was sorry to hear that. First, because I'd been hoping for a link to her grandfather's murder. And second, because I'd been with Mary through those two miscarriages, and I knew the toll a physical act, even giving birth, could have on a woman's psyche.

I promised to talk to Rick in the next day or two, and rode the rest of the way home in silence.

Chapter 24
Blinds

When Rochester and I got home from the vet, Lili was appalled at the dog's wounds. I didn't tell her what I had said to Noah. I already felt bad about it. But I was determined to fill out the police forms and collect the vet's fees from Jeffrey Lalor, even if he was bankrupt.

We drove up to Friar Lake soon after that. Eastern's trash service, which came by once a week or on demand, had already taken away the garbage, and Joey was pleased at how clean the Parents without Partners had left the property.

John William Babson, Eastern's president, arrived unexpectedly early in the afternoon. Babson, a dapper man in his late sixties, had taken a chance on me years before, offering me my first real job after my prison sentence. I worked in the college's alumni relations department for a year, along with teaching as an adjunct instructor in the English department. Then he had taken the biggest chance of all, asking me to develop and run Friar Lake.

I jumped up from my desk and greeted him. "What brings you out here today?" I asked, as Rochester sedately moved up to be petted.

"It's a beautiful day, and I had some business with Mr. Capodilupo earlier. I thought I'd come by and say hello."

We walked outside, and the bright sun and cool breeze conspired to show Friar Lake at its best. Joey's team kept the lawns a glossy, manicured green that golf courses would envy, with the occasional pop of color from yellow, red and orange zinnias. Butterflies hovered around the buddleia, and the air smelled clean and fresh.

"How's your occupancy during the summer?" Babson asked, though I was sure he already knew the answer.

"I focus on community programming while the college isn't busy," I said. "On Saturday Professor Garrett from the Philosophy Department brought over a community group of Parents Without Partners, and everyone enjoyed the facilities."

He nodded. "I've met his son. A handful, if I recall. I doubt philosophy training helps much with a small child." He smiled. "I found whenever I tried that my own children quickly outsmarted me."

Babson rarely mentioned his family. His daughter had gone to Harvard for her bachelor's and Stanford for her PhD. For a while she taught English on several native American reservations, and now she was a researcher and policy wonk in Washington DC.

He had a son as well, a few years younger, who had both a learning disability and a musical gift. As a teen, the Babsons had sent him to a residential study program in music, and from what I heard he was a brilliant violinist with a symphony orchestra somewhere.

"What else is on the agenda?" Babson asked.

"Tomorrow evening we have a presentation of a new book of photographs by Russell Wingbach. He was a friend of Lili's during her photojournalist days, and she's read the book and is excited about it. We're working in connection with an independent bookstore in Potter's Harbor as well as a gallery in New Hope that offers photography programs for adults and kids. I think it will bring an audience to Friar Lake that might not be familiar with us, or with Eastern."

"That sounds excellent. I'm glad you're collaborating with small businesses and arts organizations. I'd love to hear a concert out here sometime." He looked down at the hillside that led to the eponymous lake, and then asked, "Have you ever been to Red Rocks in Colorado?"

I shook my head. "I've seen concerts there on TV but never in person."

"My son played there a few years ago, with his orchestra. It was magnificent, and we were told the rock walls alongside the amphitheater funnel and amplify the sound. I wonder if we could do that here."

From what I'd seen of Red Rocks, it was much bigger than what we had room for. But there were natural rock formations on each side of a gently sloping hillside. "What if I get some advice from the music department?" I asked.

"Excellent idea." Babson had a faraway look in his eyes, and I wondered if he was thinking of bringing his son home to perform.

We talked about the other programs I had. We rented out our playing field to local teams, we hosted non-profit groups and also charged small fees for groups like Realtors to meet.

"You're doing a good job here, Steve," Babson said as we circled back toward the parking lot. "Friar Lake is everything I imagined we could build as a conference center, and more."

"Thank you," I said. "I couldn't do it without Joey."

"Ah, and there's another reason I wanted to come out here. We're going to be announcing a major construction project on campus soon—I can't say any more than that right now. But I have my eye on Mr. Capodilupo to manage things for me. I think he's outgrown this place."

My heart sank. Joey and I were friends, and we were a great team. "I'd be sorry to lose him. But he's a great talent."

"Yes, I think so, too. Reminds me in many ways of his father." He smiled. "Though without his dad's foul mouth—at least as far as I've seen."

"Joey's the kind of guy who gets participation by inclusion, rather than force."

"Yes, I think so too." He smiled. "Well, carry on."

I said goodbye and Rochester and I walked back to my office. I was pleased by Babson's comments, but sad to think of losing Joey. Who would I rely on when I needed to sneak out during the day to investigate something? Would Rochester like his replacement?

How could I get my golden retriever onto the hiring committee?

"Let's go see Joey."

Chapter 25
Decisions

Rochester scrambled around to his feet and was at the front door before I could get there. I hooked him up and we walked out into the warm summer sunshine.

There were no cars in the parking lot other than mine, Joey's, and the battered sedan the yard workers used, so I set him loose to run and headed toward Joey's office.

He had two buildings assigned to him—a small stone structure with his desk and file cabinets, and then a long, low building attached where he kept and repaired all the machinery that maintained the property.

When I walked in he was staring at his computer with a sad look on his face. "Babson come to see you?" I asked, as I settled into the chair across from him. Rochester went behind the desk to sit on his haunches beside Joey.

"Yeah."

"And?"

"Did he talk to you?" Joey asked.

"Sounds like a great opportunity for you."

"I don't know. I love Friar Lake—it's like my own special place. On the campus I'm just one more cog in the wheel."

"But it's a chance to build something yourself."

"Which I did here." He slumped back against his chair. "It's more money, and a lot more responsibility. Part of me says yeah, I should take this chance to move my career forward."

"And the other part?"

"I'm really happy here. I like working with you, and also having the authority to do whatever I want. Do you think I'm lazy?"

"Not at all."

"That's what my dad is going to say." Joe Capodilupo Senior had been the facilities manager for the entire college, and he had brought Joey on board as an assistant a couple of years before Friar Lake went under construction. "He wants me to move up the ranks like he did."

"He had a wife and three sons to support."

"I get that. But he also worked his ass off. I'll bet he was at Eastern ten hours a day, and on call on the weekends. What kind of a life is that?"

"It's a tough call to make. Have you spoken to Mark yet?"

Mark Figueroa owned an antique store in Stewart's Crossing, and he was one of the first people I'd met when I moved back to town. I had introduced him to Joey—dumbly, because they were both gay and tall. They'd clicked, and recently had bought a house in River Bend a few blocks from Lili and me.

"I told him that Babson offered me a promotion, and that I wanted to talk to him tonight. But I didn't tell him what it is."

"Lili and I went to that steakhouse in West Trenton on Saturday night," I said. "The one with the view of the Delaware? Why don't you guys go to dinner there and talk it over?"

He smiled. "You mean in public? So neither of us goes off the handle?"

I shrugged. "It works for me." I leaned forward. "For what it's worth, Joey, I love working with you, and I'd be happy if you and I kept managing this place together until I'm ready to retire. I think I know you, and I know you love working with the land and nature more than construction. I'm sure you'd do a great job with this new building, but honestly, I think you'd be happier here."

"That's what I'm afraid of," he said. "That I'll take the job because of the money and step up the ladder, because Mark and I can pay off our mortgage faster. But that I'll hate it and I won't be able to come back here."

"There's an extra twist you could consider," I said.

He looked up. "What?"

"You know Babson's son plays the violin, with an orchestra somewhere?"

"St. Louis, I think."

"Well, Babson and I were looking down at the lake, and he noticed the rock formations on each side of the long lawn. He thinks we could put an amphitheater there. Like Red Rocks."

"That would be so cool. Much smaller, of course, but I bet the acoustics would be great."

I stood up. "See, you could manage a project like that, stay on good terms with Babson and still keep learning and growing. The best advice I can give you is to be totally honest with Mark, and make a decision that you both agree with."

Joey knew that I'd been in prison, but he didn't know that I occasionally pulled down that laptop and darted around to places online where I didn't belong. Or that I had made a promise to Lili – that I wouldn't do anything to endanger myself, or our relationship, without checking with her first. That was the kind of agreement that kept us together, and I hoped Joey and Mark would be able to come to a similar one.

Every time I looked at Rochester I saw the bandages around his throat and I felt angry and helpless at the same time. I took him out for a run, and then back at the office opened the form Rick had emailed me. I filled out a statement about what had happened to Rochester. Then I called Rick and told him to expect the document via email. "Did you get a chance to look into if Lalor had any home health aides?" I asked.

"Interesting question. He had aides for the last year he lived in the apartment in Yardley, and then for the first year he lived with Jeffrey. Then Jeffrey canceled the contract with the agency and didn't replace them."

"Ran out of money?"

"Jeffrey was paying them out of the old man's account, which still had plenty of money by the time of his death. My guess is he was trying to hold on to his inheritance. Or leaving himself an opportunity to get rid of his father without witnesses."

"Were any of the aides named Annie Jackson?"

"Who would that be?"

I explained about the problems between Eckhardt Lalor and Annie's grandfather. "If Annie worked there, she could have learned about the rhythm of the house and when the old man would be alone. And then because Eckhardt was confused, he wouldn't complain if Annie showed up one day and wanted to take him out."

"Interesting. I'll look into it tomorrow."

At that point I gave up. I didn't have anything to do at Friar Lake and wanted to go home and spend the evening with my dog.

We rolled in a few minutes after Lili, and then she and I chose the blinds we wanted to order. "Can we ask Joey to put them up?" Lili asked.

"I have a different idea. Suppose we ask Robert Nitz to come over and give us an estimate. There are a few other things I'd like to have done at the same time, and I don't want to ask Joey for too much time."

"Who is Robert Nitz?"

"Stepson of Eckhardt Lalor. I've been trying to think of someone I could talk to about Lalor who'd have an inside scoop. Robert Nitz seems the least likely to report back to his step-siblings that I'm asking questions."

She turned to her laptop and looked up Robert Nitz. "Levitt-to-Me," she said, looking up. "I know your taste in bad puns. I can see you and Mr. Nitz will get along."

Dog's Waiting Room

"You know me too well," I said.

Chapter 26
Secret Weapon

I called Robert Nitz. "I need someone to do some drywall repair and put up new vertical blinds," I said, after hello. "Is that something you can do?"

"Sure. How did you hear about me?"

"I knew your stepfather, briefly, and I saw your truck at his funeral."

"That's as close to a recommendation as I'd ever get from the old man," he said. "I can come by this evening and look things over. Give me your address."

I did, and we agreed on six. While we waited for him, I cleaned Rochester's wounds and applied the ointment. I was pleased to see that they were already beginning to heal. It didn't make me any less angry at Sumo the Akita or his lousy family, though.

Robert Nitz arrived promptly at six. Rochester sniffed him, and approved, and then settled in the living room. "I can see why you want to replace these quickly," Robert said, as we stood in my kitchen and looked through the sliding glass doors early that evening. "Wicked sun coming through there."

He looked younger than he had appeared at the funeral, perhaps because he wore a pair of ripped jeans and a T-shirt from a motorcycle rally.

"Funny, I never noticed how strong the sun is, because it was always filtering through the blinds, and if it got too much we closed them."

"You have something in mind?"

Lili came downstairs then, and after introductions, she and I showed him the blinds that we had agreed on. "We haven't ordered them yet because we wanted to make sure they would fit."

He stood on one of our kitchen chairs to measure, which was difficult because Rochester kept snooping around. I finally had to threaten him with banishment to the upstairs if he didn't climb on the sofa and settle down.

"These'll fit," he said. "Glad you didn't order them yet, because I can get them for you at a discount. Even with a markup for my time, you'll come in cheaper if you let me place the order."

"That'd be great."

He pushed a button on his tape and it rolled shut with a snap. I showed him the few other things I needed done, and he sat at the kitchen table to put together a quick quote. He opened a folder of papers and pulled out a clean multi-part order form, scattering a few bits on the ground. "I'll get them in a minute," he said.

He filled out an order, listing the items I wanted done with an estimate for each. I signed it and gave him a check for a deposit, then said, "I have to ask, because I keep thinking about how I met your stepfather one day when he was lost, wandering along the river. Do you think someone pushed him into the Delaware?"

"If they did, more power to them," he said. "He was an evil man. But he always cloaked it behind a fake generosity. 'Look at all the homes I'm providing for poor people.'" He turned to me. "You should have seen some of those. I did. I started working for his business as soon as I graduated high school."

He reached down and picked up the papers that had spilled out of his folder. "Didn't want to, but I needed to stay on good terms with him so Susie could stay at his house and finish high school. Worked as a handyman, and he'd send me around to do minor repairs. Fix door locks, seal up leaky windows and so on. Usually only things that benefited him, or the building—not the tenants."

He shrugged. "But I tried to do what I could without him knowing. I'd stay an hour or two later than he knew, sealing up holes where rats came in, patching drywall. Painted a bunch of kids' bedrooms to give them prettier places to grow up."

"That's kind of you."

"Fat lot of good it did with him. Or with Susie either. You know she's a schoolteacher?"

I did know, but didn't want to make him think I was stalking him or his family. "Around here?"

He shook his head. "Pine Barrens. She hated growing up in Trenton, had to get out of the city. Our mother was a teacher, too, and when she died she left boxes of school supplies, visual aids, teacher stuff. Susie planned to take it all away when she got her first teaching job."

I sensed there was a but coming.

"We didn't know it, but the old man had the housekeeper clear out all her stuff within months after she died."

"That would be the housekeeper who got promoted?"

Robert laughed. "Yeah, that's what Jeff called it. She didn't last long."

"I noticed no one ever mentioned her by name, either in the obituary or at the funeral."

"Yeah, that was mean. She was the closest thing Susie and I had to a parent for a couple of years, considering the old man was always at work. Jenny. Jenny Delamare. Gosh, I haven't thought of that name for years."

The name sounded familiar, but I didn't make a quick connection, so I pushed the thought aside. We agreed he'd let me know when the blinds arrived and make a date to come install them, and he'd handle the other work then.

He left and I went upstairs, where I found Lili leaning against the headboard with her phone in front of her, and Rochester at the foot of the bed with something white between his paws.

"What have you got there, boy?" I asked, as I pried the piece of damp, slightly worn paper from him. An estimate for work to be done at Jeffrey Lalor's house.

"Where did you get this, boy?" I held it up. "Robert must have dropped it when he opened his folder. I suppose you're trying to remind me to focus on Mr. Lalor."

While Lili cooked dinner, I reapplied the ointment to Rochester's face, and then wrote up some notes for Rick. Robert's resentment of his father, and Susan's as well. But were either of them enough of a motive to kill?

Chapter 27
Stepping Out

Tuesday morning I applied more antibiotic ointment to Rochester's face, happy to see it was healing well. Then Lili joined Rochester and me in my car. Since we'd be dining that night with our guest speaker, her friend Russell Wingbach, we'd agreed it was silly to take two cars.

"I had a huge argument with Fedi last night," she said, as I backed out of the driveway. "While you and Rochester were out for your walk."

"About what?"

"He's spending so much time settling up my mother's estate, and that just brought up all those old issues, when I was traveling and he was the one who had to do everything for her."

She shifted her position so she was looking out the window. "I can't blame him, because it's the truth. I tried to call my mother once a week to check in, but sometimes I was in the middle of a war zone, or a jungle without cell service, and I couldn't always manage it."

Rochester leaned in from the back seat to rest his head on her shoulder.

"Most of the time we argued, anyway. When was I going to settle down. Why was I making her worry so much about my safety. When I could avoid talking to her I did."

She turned back to me. "Does that make me a bad daughter?"

"Of course not. You and your mother disagreed about some of the choices you made. That doesn't mean you were wrong."

"But I wasn't there when she needed help. When something broke in the condo, Fedi was the one who found someone to fix it. When she had a cancer scare, Fedi was the one who went to the doctor with her. He was the one who waited while she had her scans. He reminded me of all that last night, and I lashed out at him."

"You're siblings. You're going to fight now and then."

"But what if we can't get over this, and I lose contact with him? He's my only sibling."

"Believe me, I understand. Sometimes I wish I had a brother or sister I could talk to, who would have the same memories. But I wouldn't worry. The bond between you two is so strong. And you both have big personalities."

She crossed her arms over her chest. "Is that what you're calling it?"

"Don't get me started. You know as well as I do that you have a volcano simmering inside you. I've seen it erupt a few times. I'm sure Fedi recognizes that in you and understands it."

"Volcano," she muttered, but she turned and let Rochester lick her face, and by the time I pulled up in front of the building that housed the Fine Arts department, she was cheerful again. "See you tonight," she said, and kissed my cheek before she got out.

Joey came into my office soon after I arrived at Friar Lake. "I spoke to Mark last night about the new job," he said.

"And?"

"And of course he pushed it back on me. What do I want?"

"That is the big question, isn't it?"

He frowned, and Rochester moved over to nuzzle his leg. Or sniff for Brody. "Even my dad told me I had to decide. I was sure he was going to push me to take it."

"Why? Because that's what he did?"

Joey nodded. "He reminded me that I'm not his clone." He laughed. "As if."

"Meaning if you were his clone, you'd take the job. But you're your own person, so…"

"I was so worried I was going to lose him when he was sick," Joey said. He stood up and walked over to the big window that looked out at Friar Lake. "I wanted him to stick around and give me advice forever. Kinda pissed me off that he survived, and now he won't tell me anything."

I laughed. "He's a good dad, which you've always known."

He turned around. "Doesn't make it any easier."

"What would you do if he wasn't around to advise you?"

"Moan and complain a lot. Cry on Mark's shoulder. And eventually decide."

"So do all that. Talk out your options. Make sure you figure out which ones matter to you. And then decide."

I stood up. "Come on, Rochester and I will walk you back to your office."

As Rochester romped ahead of us, I said, "I never had the chance to make big decisions myself," I said. "When I was a senior at Eastern, I applied to law schools and graduate schools in English, because there didn't seem to be anything else I could do with a bachelor's degree. I didn't get into any decent law schools, but I got accepted at Columbia for an MA in English. So I let that make the decision for me."

Rochester grabbed a stick in his mouth and began running in circles around us. "Then when I was at Columbia, I met Mary, and I started teaching as an adjunct at a couple of places in the city because one of my professors told me I should, and helped me apply."

"But you like teaching, don't you?"

I shrugged. "As well as anything else. Then Mary got a promotion and a transfer to California, and we got married because that way her company would cover my moving with her."

"Really? That's why you got married?"

"Well, I thought I loved her, and she loved me, and it seemed obvious, you know? The world aligning." We stopped outside the door to Joey's office in one of the old abbey outbuildings. "And then her miscarriages happened, and I didn't think about what I was doing with the hacking, and then the state of California told me what to do for the next year."

Rochester dropped his stick and ran over to us and squatted beside me. I reached down and patted his head. "My father died, and he left me the house, so it was obvious that I should move back here. I didn't see any way to start over again out there, with my record. No one I knew would ever hire me."

"But you ended up at Eastern. You had to make that decision."

I shrugged. "I tried to start up a technical writing business, and that failed. I taught a couple of courses as an adjunct, and then President Babson took an interest in me. He's the one who gave me a full-time job in the alumni office, and then he's the one who pushed me to come out here."

"The way he's pushing me."

"Yup. Only you have options, when I didn't. I was working in the alumni office for the length of the capital campaign, and when that finished I was going to be out of a job. If I wanted to stay employed, and avoid job hunting with a criminal record, I had to take this on."

I turned to him. "Don't get me wrong, I'm incredibly grateful that he mentored me and pushed me. I'm happy here. If it wasn't for him I don't know what I'd be doing. Struggling from one dead-end job to another. Working fast food or waiting tables. I'd probably never have met Lili. Or you, or Mark, or any of my other friends."

I put my hand on his shoulder, reaching up because he was so much taller than I was. "You have options. You get to choose which job you want based on what you enjoy."

"I really love it out here," he said. "The woods that need managing, the lawns and the flowers. Using all my handyman skills to keep everything working. It's my own domain, and I'm so fortunate I can be outdoors and doing physical things one minute, then inside forcing my brain to work the next."

"Sounds like you've already made your choice."

He took a deep breath. "I have. I'm just having a hard time facing it. And thinking about what President Babson and my father will say."

"I have known John William Babson for a long time," I said. "He was the president when I was a student here, remember? And there's one thing he's been consistent about. Helping every student reach their potential, setting them on a path to a life of happiness and service and productivity. I think he'll be happy that you know what you want."

"And my dad?"

"He's already told you, hasn't he? He wants you, and Mark, to be happy."

He reached around and hugged me. "Thanks, Steve. I really hope we can keep working together for a long time."

"Me, too," I said.

Later that day, Rochester and I waited for Lili and Russell Wingbach at a brewpub called Station Ten, in the former fire station of that number.

Rochester spotted Lili and a man I recognized as Wingbach approaching, and I had to hold his collar to keep him from rushing forward to greet her and sniff him. Wingbach was in his seventies, with a mane of white hair and skin that showed the effects of a life outdoors.

She introduced us, and I said, "We have one of your photos on the wall in our living room. Jackson Hole at sunrise, the town just waking up with that huge mountain behind it. It speaks to me about how much greater the power of nature is than the petty affairs of men."

"Well, thank you. I do tend to look for landscapes that have a deeper meaning. I've been called an overthinking Ansel Adams."

He had a messenger bag over his shoulder, and as he transferred it to the back of a chair, he picked something out.

"I brought you a little gift," he said, handing Lili a flat package. It was wrapped in brown kraft paper with a large photo-sticker on it of an eagle in flight.

"The eagle is Russel's spirit animal," she said to me. "At least that's what an old Tlingit woman told him."

"I took that photo and printed it on sticky paper," he said. "And voila! I have stickers for every purpose."

Lili opened the package carefully, preserving the eagle sticker, and she pulled out a simple picture frame. When she turned it over she gasped.

It was a photo of her and her mother on the beach in Florida. "It's... it's..." she started to say, and then she began crying. Rochester sat up and put his head on her knee, and she stroked the soft fur there.

"Lili's mother passed away a couple of weeks ago," I explained.

"I'm so sorry," Russell said. "I spotted a run of photos I took a few years ago, when I ran into you in Miami with your mother, and this was the best of the lot."

The sun was setting behind them, illuminating strands of Lili's auburn hair like she was in a Renaissance painting. Benita, too, was at her fieriest, staring at the camera as if daring Russell to take her picture.

"I didn't realize you look so much alike," I said. I'd been distracted by Benita's black bouffant, the way she used makeup so much more than Lili. But in the photo I saw the similarity in their heart-shaped faces. More than that, I could see similar strength in both women.

"It's magnificent, Russell," Lili said. "The way you posed us, the way you caught the light. My god, I could lecture for an hour on composition and chiaroscuro."

"Please don't," Russell and I both said at the same time, and we all laughed.

"When was this?" I asked.

"The summer before I started teaching at Eastern as an adjunct. Six years ago. When I was traveling so much, my mother let me keep some things with her, and I went down to choose what I wanted to have packed up and sent here."

She turned to me. "Do you know, that apartment in Leighville was the first permanent home I had by myself? When I was twenty, I left the dorm for Adriano's apartment. After that marriage ended I shared places for years until I married Philip and moved into his co-op. And after that divorce I was always on assignment and never kept a place."

"So no chance you could turn into a hoarder like your mother."

"No. And then I lasted on my own what, two years, before I moved in with you?"

"I did the same thing but in reverse," Russell said. "I married excellent housekeepers. Each one of them kept the house after we divorced."

We laughed, and ordered. I kept to one beer because I was driving, but Lili and Russell drank several rounds of saketinis, a cocktail of sake and gin, apparently in memory of a wild party in Tokyo many years before.

Lili had become so accustomed to standing behind the camera that she had cultivated an ability to fit into the background of any setting. But she was lucky that liquor accelerated everything good about her—she was less inhibited, so her natural wit and creativity blossomed. She and Russell told great stories. I had to push them to finish dinner so we could make it back to Friar Lake in time for Russell to read from the introduction to his new book of photos, and show some slides.

Joey was already there to open the building, and Mark had saved seats for Lili and me in the front row of the chapel. Russell was waylaid by the gallery owner from New Hope and her coterie, and I was pleased to see some familiar faces, including a group of friends from Potter's Harbor, the town on the Delaware just downhill from Leighville.

I had taught as an adjunct with Naomi Schechter, a short, funny woman with a red beret and red-framed glasses, and through her knew her girlfriend Anne Marie, who loved books of fashion photography. With them was Naomi's best gay friend, a one-time Eastern professor named Jeff Berman, who had a new book coming out and also a gig with a true-crime podcast.

Lili introduced Russell, and he began with a slide show of some of his most famous photographs, and then some that had special meaning to him. He surprised Lili by including the picture of her and her mother. Mark, next to her, grabbed her hand and squeezed when it came up on the screen.

Russell told stories in between pictures, and his last photo was one of a woman with wild blonde hair pointing a gun at him. There was a whole story to be examined in her eyes alone, which were open wide, bloodshot, yet terrifyingly focused on him. "My third ex-wife, Beatrice," he said. "Right before she shot me."

Rochester, who had been lying peacefully at my feet, suddenly sat up at attention as the audience gasped.

"This might have been the last photo I ever took," Russell said. "Except that Beatrice was a lousy shot, even when sober, and this was taken after we'd each snorted several lines of cocaine."

"She hit me in the shoulder, and I dropped my camera to the marble floor. A Hasselblad 500 C. It smashed, and at first that was all I cared about. I dropped to my knees and tried to pick it up, and that's when I felt the pain in my arm for the first time."

He shook his head. "That was one of my favorite cameras, too."

The audience laughed, but I could tell they were eager, as I was, to hear what came next.

"I learned something important that night," Russell continued. "Of course, I'd always known that I used the camera as a screen against feelings. What I hadn't realized was how much I disliked each of the women I'd married. I was always a spectator, even at my own wedding ceremonies. By the time the police arrived to take Beatrice into custody and put me in an ambulance, I resolved to step in front of the camera more and be a part of my own real, authentic life."

He stepped out from behind the podium and bowed to the audience. "And here I am."

The crowd roared with approval, and after a round of questions from the audience, the gallery owner swept Russell away to follow her in his rental car to his hotel in New Hope. Lili, Rochester and I walked outside.

"What did you think?" I asked Lili.

"Like the photograph, there's a lot for me to consider," she said. Then she stopped and turned to face me. "Do you think we both hide from each other sometimes? Me behind the camera, you behind a computer screen?"

"I wouldn't call it hiding," I said. "I think in any healthy relationship, the couple needs time together, and time apart. It's good that we each have our own interests."

She nodded. "And do you think I'm fully present, when I'm not taking photographs?"

"That depends on what you mean by fully present. When you focus on me, absolutely. I feel connected to you. But I know you have a lot of other roles in life—daughter, sister, teacher, administrator, photographer. I don't mind being with you when you're focused on one of those."

I put my left arm through hers, held Rochester's leash with my right hand, and we moved on through the darkness, our way illuminated by the stars above and the occasional streetlamp in the Friar Lake parking lot.

Chapter 28
A Long Wait

That night, as I walked Rochester through the shadowy streets of River Bend, I remembered how he had sat up when Russell Wingbach told the story of being shot. It was probably the tension that his announcement caused in the audience that alerted him.

Wingbach had three ex-wives, just like Eckhardt Lalor. Wingbach's third wife had tried to kill him. Had Lalor's third done the same thing, and been successful? Had Rick considered Genevieve Lalor? They'd been divorced for a long time, but resentments often go very deep.

By the time we returned to the house all those saketinis had caught up to Lili and she'd gone to sleep. I set up the ladder and climbed up a couple of steps, and retrieved the hacker laptop from its accustomed spot. Then I sat at the kitchen table to see what I could find about Eckhardt Lalor's third wife, the one who had been "promoted" from housekeeper, to quote Jeffrey. Did she, or someone connected with her, have a grudge against the old man?

I did a quick dive into the dark web, where I found the software I needed. I took the steps necessary to protect myself from detection, and then felt justified in my efforts because the very first site I tried came up with three marriage licenses for Eckhardt Lalor. Marie Innocenza in 1953. Jane Turpin Nitz in 1980, and Genevieve Delamare in 1982.

I did the same search for divorces and found that Eckhardt and Genevieve Lalor had divorced in 1987. Divorces were public records, and ones filed before 1999 could be accessed at the court where they were filed or at a Federal Records Center.

The Lalors had chosen New Hampshire, the quickest place in the US to get a divorce, where the minimum filing time is less than a day. The state's records were online in an automated system called NHVRIN, and my fingers began to tingle. The site was for authorized users only, though, and there was a bold warning on the home page: "Any or all uses of this system and all files on this system may be intercepted, monitored, recorded, copied, audited, inspected, and disclosed to authorized site and law enforcement personnel, as well as authorized officials of other agencies both domestic and foreign."

That was the kind of language that made me excited.

Rochester came to stand beside me, nuzzling my leg. It was as if he was trying to keep me from the computer. I calculated the risks and found, more than anything, that I wanted to do this. My spidey-senses were tingling, as if they knew there was some juicy information to be found online.

It was like hacking Jeffrey Lalor's security camera. I didn't harm him or his family by what I did. And it wouldn't hurt them if I got this information I needed.

Rochester thrust himself up so he was resting on my thigh, keeping my hands away from the keyboard. I started to push him away, but then I stopped. Was this something I should pass by Lili or Rick before I did it?

And then I knew. They'd both tell me not to do it, not when Rick, as a law enforcement officer, could make a legal request for the information. I was impatient, seized by the desire to hack.

I took a couple of deep breaths, and petted Rochester's head. Then I pushed him gently away and positioned my hands on the keyboard. I wrote up what I had learned and emailed Rick, and asked him if he could get the records of Lalor's divorce. I didn't know if Genevieve Delamare Lalor was a suspect, and there was no reason why I couldn't wait to find out the conditions of her divorce.

Then I sat back and considered what I had. Lots of people had motive to kill Eckhardt Lalor, from his family to Annie Jackson, to anyone who'd felt cheated by his company's poor maintenance of their housing. But who had done it? Despite all the research I'd done, I was no closer to a solution, and it was frustrating.

When you add to that my anger over the attack on Rochester, I was boiling. But what else could I do?

Rick texted as Rochester and I were out for our late-night walk, and I arranged to meet him the next morning at the Chocolate Ear.

When Rochester and I came back from our walk, Lili was in the living room, trying to find a place to hang the photo Russell Wingbach had given her. The problem was that it was relatively small, only eight by ten, and you had to get close to it to appreciate it.

"I should buy a nicer frame," she said, frowning. "Or I could ask Russell for the negative and have it blown up."

I reorganized a couple of golden retriever knickknacks on the bookshelf, including a sign that read, *Beware of the dog: He will steal your heart.* "Put it there," I said. "Eye level, and right next to the one you took of me and Rochester."

That photo was one of my favorites. Rochester and I were on the sofa together, and Lili snapped the shot just as he turned and licked my face, and my mouth opened in surprise.

She stepped back, analyzed, then nodded. "Perfect."

She took my hand and we walked upstairs together, her arm trailing behind her as she kept hold of me. We had to close the bedroom door on Rochester, which made him unhappy, but on rare occasions I did what I wanted, not necessarily what was best for him. And I wanted Lili.

I let him back in the bedroom a while later, while Lili was brushing her teeth, and he jumped right up and sniffed the covers, then settled down in the middle of the bed.

Because I was meeting Rick, I stuck to a piece of toast and jam for breakfast. While Lili read the news on her iPad, I went over the suspects I wanted to talk to Rick about: Genevieve Lalor, Annie Jackson, and Susan Nitz. He was already in the café when Rochester and I arrived, and with a café mocha and a chocolate croissant for me and a biscuit for Rochester.

He was really serious when he pulled out his notebook. "We had a break yesterday. The neighbor across the street was down the shore for vacation and didn't find my card in her door until she and her husband got home Sunday evening."

He sipped his coffee. "The day Lalor died, she was home all day packing and baking stuff for her grandkids. Her kitchen window looks out at the street, and she remembers seeing the old man go out in the early afternoon with a woman."

"A woman. That narrows your suspect list considerably. She remember anything more about her?"

"Just the impression that the woman was an aide, and she was happy that Jeffrey had hired one again."

"An aide. Uniform?"

Rick shook his head. "I think she's basing her impression on the car the woman was driving. An old SUV, one of the smaller models, with damage to the trunk."

"Any chance it was Anita Lalor? Would the neighbor know her by sight?"

"I checked Anita's alibi again. She and both her brothers were in a meeting at the company office in Hamilton Township that day. The company lawyer, accountant and head of leasing were all in with them, and confirmed that all three remained in the meeting during the time Eckhardt Lalor went missing."

"Did you get a chance to check out Annie Jackson?"

"The home health aide? On an assignment in Lawrenceville. According to the agency, her time sheet says she arrived there at eight AM and stayed until six, when the night shift aide signed in. I called the client, and she's very sharp, though she just had both her hips replaced so she can't get around much. She confirmed that Annie was with her all day."

He looked up at me and smiled. "Apparently she's a hawk when it comes to time sheets. Complains if the girls are more than a few minutes late, and won't let them leave during the day unless there's a replacement. Even told me, 'I get what I pay for!'"

"Annie's out of the running, then. Any other female suspects at the top of the list?"

Rick shook his head. "I feel like I'm back to square one."

"Maybe I can help there. I have two more to consider." I nibbled on my croissant and followed with a sip of coffee. "Robert Nitz was over my house Monday to give me a quote on replacing that valance over the kitchen doors. There was a leak a few years ago that softened the drywall and it collapsed."

"Everybody okay?"

"Rochester was the most spooked. But I called Robert Nitz, who has a handyman business, to come over and take a look. We got to talking, and he mentioned his sister Susan had a real grudge against their stepfather. He threw away a lot of stuff that she was supposed to inherit from her mother."

Rick frowned. "Is that a motive?"

"Does she have an alibi?" I countered.

He flipped through his notes while I had some more coffee. "Hmm. She's a third-grade teacher in Hammonton, NJ. School was in session that day, but that's as far as I've checked."

"OK. I have one more for you. Genevieve Delamare Lalor."

"The third wife?"

I felt deflated. "You knew about her?"

"Duh. Of course." Rick picked up his coffee and sipped it, as if he had something to tell me but he was making me wait. "I requested the conditions of her divorce from Lalor from the state of New Hampshire." He pulled an envelope out of his shirt pocket. "This came in today's mail. Haven't had a chance to look at it yet."

He handed me the envelope and I opened it. "I almost got this myself," I said.

"By got you mean..."

"I thought about hacking in. I have a piece of software that promises easy access to state government sites."

I pulled the letter out of the envelope. "But I didn't. I **am** learning, you know."

"Good. Anything interesting in the divorce papers?"

I scanned the page. "Genevieve was the petitioner, and she alleged that not only was Eckhardt unfaithful to her, he infected her with a sexually transmitted disease."

"Ouch. You know the difference between love and herpes?"

"Herpes is forever. But he gave her HPV." I picked up my phone. "Do I need to Google that?"

"Human papillomavirus. Most commonly transmitted STD these days. Usually harmless and goes away in a few days, but it can in some cases lead to genital warts and cancer. More common in teens and younger women."

"You know a lot about this."

"Police department required videos. The divorce was over twenty years ago. How old was Lalor then?" He pulled out his notebook. "He would have been in his fifties then. Cheating on his younger wife with someone who was probably even younger."

"A hound dog. Wouldn't surprise me if it was one of his tenants." I looked back at the document. "Lalor admitted fault and gave Genevieve a lump sum payment of $100,000. She agreed that she would not disclose the terms of the divorce with anyone else, specifically not any member of Lalor's family."

Rick sipped his coffee. "But she divorced him back in 1987. Why wait 27 years to get back at him?"

I shrugged and looked down at Rochester. He didn't have anything to contribute. "Does she have an alibi?"

"Don't know. Didn't talk to her, because she was so much in the past."

"Maybe Lalor was fooling around with younger women while he was married to Genny, and afterwards. Maybe there's an illegitimate child out there who wanted revenge, or thought he or she would inherit something."

"I think you're straying into fantasyland."

"Got anything better?"

He groaned. "No. But I'll see what I can find."

We finished our coffee and stood up. "I'm glad you resisted that impulse," Rick said. "It would be awkward if I had to arrest my best friend."

"Guess so," I said.

Chapter 29
Making Amends

Rochester and I drove up to Friar Lake, where we were hosting a monthly luncheon for the local Realtors' association. I kept busy opening the kitchen for the two older women from Eastern's dining service, who put together salad and a buffet of tortillas and fillings. I helped with the cleanup, using the opportunity to snag some chopped chicken for Rochester, and then spent the rest of the afternoon with him at my feet as I signed purchase orders and answered emails.

Late in the afternoon, Jeffrey Lalor called me. "I want to apologize for Sumo's behavior, and give you a check to cover your vet bills," he said.

"That's good of you."

"You don't live far from here, do you? I'd love it if you could come over this evening and Noah can apologize in person, and we can show you that Sumo can be a good loving dog when he's properly introduced."

I had to admit I was curious. And I probably owed Noah an apology for my outburst by the river, especially as the neighbor had told Rick it was a woman who'd taken Eckhardt out for his final ride.

"Sure. How about seven o'clock?"

We agreed, and I hung up. I looked over at Rochester, and the puncture marks were hardly visible and the chance of infection was gone. I needed to get over my anger and move on.

When I got home that evening, Lili was on the phone with Fedi again, and even though I couldn't understand most of the Spanish, I understood the tone. She laughed several times, and then she said, "*Buenas noches, mi amor.* I'll talk to you tomorrow."

"Fedi?" I asked.

"No, my new Spanish boyfriend." She laughed and poked me. "You were right, we're getting along better now that most of the paperwork is done. I feel like I've gotten my little brother back, the one I could talk to and play with for hours on end."

"I made up with Jeffrey Lalor, too," I said. "I'm going over there later to pick up a check for Rochester's medical bills."

"That's good. I'll pay extra special attention to Rochester while you're gone."

I drove out to Crossing Estates after dinner. It was a few days until the summer solstice, so the sun was still quite bright. I walked up to the front door, and Noah answered.

"Mr. Levitan," he said. "I'm so sorry about what happened to your dog."

"He's healing," I said. "I need to apologize to you for what I said. I was angry."

"It's okay. I'd be really upset if anything happened to Sumo."

I followed him inside, where we found his father in the living room. He stood up and greeted me, and Noah went to get Sumo. I handed him a copy of the vet bill, which totaled $165.00 between the visit and the tests, and he said, "There'll be follow up, too. Why don't I round the check up to two hundred?"

I agreed that was generous, and he wrote the check and handed it to me. Then Noah walked in with Sumo on a short leash. I had to admit he was a beautiful dog. He had a wedge-shaped head, prick ears, and rectangular body. For the most part, his coat was the same golden color as Rochester's, though he had a white patch that ran from under his neck all the way down to his paws. His back legs were white, too, and he had a lovely gold tail that curled back on itself.

I held my hand out to him, and he licked it.

"See, he's a good boy," Noah said earnestly.

I rubbed Sumo behind his ears the way Rochester liked, and he opened his mouth in a wide grin. "I'm glad you're taking care of him," I said.

I looked up at the wall, where someone had done a good job of framing family pictures. "Vivian did that," Jeffrey said. "She has a great eye for design."

I scanned down the line, a random organization of kids at all different ages and in different combinations. Now that I had met all Lalor's adult children, it was interesting to pick them out when they were younger. Jeffrey was tall, Anita smiling, Peter often looking at something outside the frame.

There was a big shot that had almost a *Sound of Music* quality to it. Eckhardt Lalor to one side, and all the kids in height order, ending in a young woman I didn't recognize, with a cigarette dangling from her fingertips. I looked closer at it.

"That's the last photo we have of all the kids together with my dad," Jeffrey said.

"Who's the woman at the end?" She looked familiar but I couldn't place her.

"Jenny. Dad hired her to be the housekeeper but he had a problem..." He looked over at his son, as if unwilling to say anything in front of him.

"Keeping it in his pants," Noah finished for him.

"Yeah, that," Jeffrey said. "She accused him of cheating a couple of years into the marriage and walked out."

That matched what Rick had found in the divorce paperwork. When a couple is monogamous, there's no chance of either getting an STD, and Lalor had as much as admitted he'd cheated when he signed the decree and paid off Jenny.

"The younger kids kept in touch with her for a while, but I

haven't heard anything in years," Jeffrey said. "The way she smoked, she's probably dead of lung cancer by now."

With a flash of insight, I realized she wasn't, though. She was serving customers at the Fiddler's Creek Lodge in West Trenton.

I left Crossing Estates a few minutes later, but I only drove as far as the lay-by on the River Road before I pulled over and called Rick.

"Have you tracked down Jenny Lalor yet?" I asked.

"She's not an easy woman to find. She's changed her name a couple of times—from Delamare to Lalor and back again. In some places she's listed as Genevieve, others Jenny with a J and still others Genny with a G. I've got a whole list of places to check on for her, but I had to give a presentation at the high school today."

"I know where she is. She's waiting tables at the Fiddler's Creek Lodge."

"How'd you find that out?"

I told him about my visit with Lili, and the outburst by the server that night. "The manager called her Genevieve, so I didn't make the connection at the time. But I was just at Jeffrey Lalor's..."

Rick interrupted me. "I asked you not to go yell at the guy."

"And I didn't. He invited me over to apologize and give me a check for Rochester's vet bills. While I was there I saw an old family photo on the wall, from the time when Genevieve was the housekeeper. I recognized her."

"Fiddler's Creek Lodge?" he asked. "I'll have to check that out tomorrow."

"The manager said that she was in a lot of pain. Maybe the HPV that Lalor gave her has caught up with her, after all this time, and she went back to Lalor to get more money."

"Possibly. I'll call her in tomorrow and let you know how it works out."

I turned back onto the River Road. It made sense that Genevieve would come back to her ex-husband if she had cancer, or something else that could be traced back to the HPV. She might have asked for money for treatment, or a lump of cash so she could quit her job and focus on her health.

But what if Eckhardt Lalor was so confused that he didn't remember her? I'd already seen her temper break out at the restaurant. Was she the mystery woman escorting Lalor into a car the day he died?

Chapter 30
Arm in Arm

Friday passed lazily at Friar Lake. It seemed like the bees were the only ones who were busy. I had no events scheduled that day, and when Rick called and asked me to meet him at the Chocolate Ear that afternoon I was eager to accommodate him.

"I have Genevieve Lalor coming in at three o'clock, before her shift at the restaurant. I want to see what I can get out of her and then bounce it off you."

"Consider me your bounce house," I said.

Rochester and I ducked out of Friar Lake around two-thirty, because I was too eager to meet with Rick and couldn't focus on anything at work. The weather had turned unseasonably cool for June, with a nice breeze sweeping down from the north, so we picked one of the wrought-iron tables on Main Street, in the shade of the Chocolate Ear's dark green awning.

I settled in with a café mocha, and Rochester got one of Gail's special biscuits. I sank into a kind of reverie, watching the traffic going up and down Main Street. Mostly SUVs and luxury cars, not the station wagons and plebeian sedans of my youth, but the moms were still young and tired-looking, the kids happy to be out of school.

I was staring into space, facing toward the police station, when a woman came into view, racing toward me. By the time she got close enough that I could recognize Genevieve Lalor, she was panting heavily, with strands of blonde hair plastered to her sweaty face.

I stood up and gently took her arm. She was staggering by then, and I guided her into the seat across from me. "Take it easy, Jenny," I said. "You look like you're exhausted."

"I can't keep on like this," she said, as she slumped into the chair. Rochester sat up next to her and sniffed her encouragingly. She reached down to pet him, but began coughing heavily and he slunk back beneath the chair.

I looked inside and caught Gail's eye, and waved to her, then pointed to Jenny. Gail got the message, and was outside a moment later with a plastic tumbler of ice water.

Jenny took a couple of long draws as Gail went back inside.

"What's the matter, Jenny? Are you sick?"

"The bastard gave me cancer. All these years it's been inside me, waiting until I get old to jump out, like the alien in that movie."

"The HPV turned into cancer?"

She nodded. "That's what the doctor says. It started in my lungs and now it's everywhere."

"I'm so sorry," I said.

I was so focused on Jenny that I didn't notice Rick coming up behind her, until he pulled another of the wrought-iron chairs over to join us.

"Why'd you run away, Ms. Lalor?" he asked.

"I felt terrible after I did it. I still do. I didn't want to have to go through it all with you again."

"I'm sorry, but you're going to have to," Rick said.

"Why don't you start with going to the doctor," I suggested. Rick frowned, but he sat back in his seat to listen.

"I don't like doctors," Jenny said defiantly. "Always telling me to stop smoking, like I don't already know it's bad for me. But I have to have something, you know."

I nodded encouragingly.

"But then I got this damn cough," she said, and as if on cue she began coughing again. I waited until she caught her breath, then passed her the tumbler of water, beads of condensation dripping slowly down its sides.

"They never want to tell you anything straight out. Oh, we have to do this test, and that test. I got insurance from the Lodge, but the co-pays and deductibles started to mount up until they finally told me the news. Metastatic lung cancer, they said. They could give me chemotherapy to try and slow the growth, maybe reduce the size of the tumors. But it's expensive, all those treatments, time in the hospital, weeks off work. I couldn't manage it."

"So you went to your ex-husband for help," I said.

She nodded. "Eckhardt was a louse, but he was generous to me in the divorce settlement. He was old. There was no reason why he couldn't give some of his money to me, instead of to all those children, who've been getting it all their lives."

"You drive an SUV?" I asked.

She pointed across the street. "That beat-up old Suzuki over there." She peered at me. "Who are you again?"

"Steve Levitan." I hesitated. "I knew Eckhardt Lalor."

"Then you knew what a bastard he could be. I know one of his neighbors through the restaurant—an older woman, older than me, who's sick, too. I baked a cake for her and took it over there. And that got me past security."

She smiled. I could see she was a smart woman, simply driven past endurance.

"Then I went to see Eck. The bastard pretended not to recognize me."

"He was suffering from Alzheimer's," I said gently. "When I met him he'd forgotten his own name."

She turned the corner of her mouth up in a sneer. "You don't know Eck. That was just another one of his tricks. But I played along. I reminded him that I was married to him, and that while we were married he was screwing around and he caught the HPV virus."

She drank some more water. "Back then, he was worried about what people would say if the truth got out, the Elks and the Lions and the Ky-wannis. He promised me that he would take care of me if anything happened."

She started to cry. "The doctors say that's what's caused my cancer now, the HPV. It's at the back of the throat, my tongue and my tonsils."

She pulled a cigarette from a pack in her pocket and lit it. "Course these don't help any, they say. But Eck kept refusing to say he knew me. I even showed him one of the pictures on the wall, me with all his kids. 'That was the housekeeper,' he said. 'I had to fire her.'"

On the ground beneath her, I saw Rochester make the same move he had at the restaurant when the smoke got to him. He leaned his head to the pavement and put his right paw above his mouth. I felt bad for him but I didn't want Genevieve to stop talking.

She took a long drag on her cigarette. "You can imagine that infuriated me. To pretend I was never even married to him." She sneered again. "I looked at him, how old and frail he was. Even sick as I am I could force him to agree. So I told him we were going for a ride."

"He agreed?" I asked. I noticed Rick hanging back, though his phone was on the table and I figured he was recording us.

"I told him we'd go past the old house by Cadwalader Park. He said he missed that place. But instead I took him out to the Delaware. I knew from years ago that he couldn't swim. I figured that if he wasn't going to give me some money, I'd get whatever I was owed in his will."

"What did you do, Genevieve?" I asked. "But I have to tell you, if you admit to something then I'm bound to tell the police what you told me."

"I put my arm in his, just like we used to walk through Cadwalader Park. Right down to the edge of the river where I saw there was a strong current. And then I let him go."

"You pushed him in the river?" I asked.

"I did. And I stood there and watched him flail around for a couple of minutes until he finally sunk under the water and the current picked him up and took him downstream."

Then her voice rose into a wail. "You didn't know him! What a rat bastard he was, pretending to rent out safe apartments when they were really death traps. How miserable he was to me and his own kids. And they're all just like him! The world is better off without him."

Rick stood up and pulled a pair of handcuffs off his belt. "It's time for you to come back to the station, Genevieve."

She launched herself at Rick, fists pummeling him, and Rochester jumped up between them, up on his hind paws with his front ones on her chest. She hit him a couple of times but there was no force in her blows by then, and she was coughing again.

This time Rick hooked the cuffs before he spoke. "Genevieve Lalor, I'm arresting you for the murder of Eckhardt Lalor."

Chapter 31
Beauty

"I'd appreciate it if you left Rochester out of this one," Rick said, as he prepared to walk away with Genevieve. "I'd be embarrassed to say that dog saved my bacon yet again."

We drove home, and I found Lili in the kitchen making one of her mother's recipes. "How was your day?" she asked.

"Interesting. Creepy, scary."

She stopped stirring to look at me. "Talk."

I told her about planning to meet Rick at the Chocolate Ear, but how Genevieve Lalor had come running down Main Street and I'd stopped her. "I got her to sit down and calm down, and then Rick showed up and eventually she told us the whole story. About getting HPV from Lalor, how years later it turned into cancer. She wanted money from him for treatment, but he'd forgotten who she was."

"That's awful." Her eyes got a faraway look in them for a moment.

"Who's more likely?" I asked. "Philip or Adriano?"

"It's scary sometimes how we can read each other's minds," Lili said. "Honestly, I think Philip is the one most likely to forget about me if he gets dementia. There were a number of students before me, and I'm sure a number after."

"That smells so good," I said, sniffing the air. "What is it?"

"*Arroz imperial*," she said. "Chicken with rice."

"Isn't that *arroz con pollo*?"

"It's a dressed-up version, layered with cheese like a lasagna."

My stomach grumbled. "And when will this delectable delight be ready?"

"I'm almost ready to start assembling it and then it has to bake for about twenty minutes. Why don't you take Rochester for a walk while you wait?"

Rochester came up to us then, with a piece of paper in his mouth. I pried it out and realized it was the business card for the manager at Fiddler's Creek Lodge. "Good clue," I said to him. "You were telling me to look back at the restaurant and that waitress. You're right, you know? Just a little late on this one."

We strolled up Sarajevo Way and made a couple of turns, then I realized we were at the house Joey and Mark had bought a few months earlier. As we passed, I heard Brody, their English cream golden, barking, and Rochester tugged me toward the front door.

I saw that Joey's truck was in the driveway, so I let Rochester lead me, but I rang the bell for him.

Joey answered the door in a T-shirt and denim shorts, holding a hammer. Brody rushed between his legs and leapt onto Rochester. "Brody, no!" Joey said, but that was pretty ineffectual. He stood back. "Come on in."

I let Rochester off his leash and the two dogs disappeared into the house in a blur of gold and white. "I didn't mean to disturb you," I said. "We were walking and Brody must have smelled Rochester and started barking."

"It's OK. A couple of the wood floor tiles came loose and I just finished hammering them back into place. You want a beer?"

"That would be nice." I followed him into the kitchen. "Mark's not home?"

"The antique store's open until eight tonight. I'm going to pick up sandwiches for us later and take them over there. He has some stuff he wants me to fix for him."

He opened the fridge and pulled out a couple of Dogfish Head SeaQuench Ales for us. I'd introduced him to the brand, as I had Rick, and we'd all become dedicated customers. Suckers for anything dog-related, I guess.

"After you left, I closed up Friar Lake and drove into Leighville," Joey said. "Met with President Babson."

"And?"

"I told him that I was honored that he thought of me for this new job, but that I'm happy with where I am."

"How did he take it?"

"I was surprised. He told me that he thought I'd want to stay at Friar Lake, but he wanted to give me the opportunity. He said something about that amphitheater again, and that you and I make a great team, and great teams need to be celebrated."

I felt a flush of pleasure. It was always nice to hear that your boss thought you were doing a good job.

"I thought we'd celebrate this weekend. Can you, Lili and Rochester come over for dinner tomorrow night? You can see what we're doing with the house, and Rochester can play with Brody, who is getting incredibly spoiled and needs a bigger dog to boss him around for a while."

We looked across the room, where Brody was chasing Rochester. He was almost as big as my dog, and as he aged he'd gotten golden streaks in his fur. "I doubt Rochester can do that, but as long as Lili hasn't made other plans we'd be delighted to come."

Grudgingly, Rochester gave up playing with Brody and we walked home, though he got over his resentment when I fed him bits of chicken thighs from Lili's dish. She was happy to have dinner with Joey and Mark the next night, and promised to make her mother's rum cake recipe, heavily dosed with some Bacardi Club she'd brought back from her mother's cupboard.

As I relaxed with a book, Rick called. "I met with Jeffrey Lalor this evening to go over the resolution to his father's murder. He was stunned that Jenny held a grudge for so long."

"People do hold onto grudges. Especially against someone who caused them to get cancer."

"Yeah. Apparently Jeffrey is reconciling with his ex-wife. Her company is buying the technology from his, and Lalor is going to sell the house in Crossing Estates and move out to Silicon Valley to help with the transition."

"Good. Maybe that means Vivian will pay Noah's tuition at Harvey Mudd."

"Wouldn't know about that. But I did meet the dog that attacked Rochester. Big bruiser. Apparently he still has some marks on his neck where you twisted his collar."

"I'd do it again, in a heartbeat. Nobody messes with my dog on my watch."

"I hear you, brother. I feel the same way."

As we prepared for bed, Lili and I talked about taking a vacation week down the shore, just the three of us. "I'm still sorting out how I feel about my mother," she said. "I could use some long walks by the beach, lots of swimming, some candlelight dinners."

"Sounds good to me. Next week?"

"Can you get away?"

I shrugged. "As long as Joey is there to make sure the place doesn't burn down. And he's passing on that promotion, and going to stick with me."

"How could he not?" Lili asked. "He must see the same things in you that I do."

"Or it's Rochester." When he heard his name, my big happy golden rose up from his place on the floor to stand beside me and nuzzle my knee. "Who could pass up the chance to spend his days with this beauty?"

"Indeed," Lili said.

Thanks for reading! There's another Golden Retriever Mystery in the pipeline—All *Dog's Children*. You can hear about it when it's ready through my newsletter or Facebook page.

I'd love to stay in touch with you. Subscribe to one or more of my newsletters, Gay Mystery and Romance or Golden Retriever Mysteries, via my website, www.mahubooks.com and I promise I won't spam you!

Follow me at Goodreads to see what I'm reading, and my author page at Facebook where I post news and giveaways.

If you liked this book, please consider posting a brief review at your vendor, at Goodreads and in reader groups. Even a short review help other readers discover books they might like. And there are often specific vendor promotions I can sign up for, only if I have a certain number of reviews posted at the vendor. Thanks!

Here is the series in order:

1. In Dog We Trust
2. Kingdom of Dog
3. Dog Helps Those
4. Dog Bless You
5. Whom Dog Hath Joined
6. Dog Have Mercy
7. Honest to Dog
8. Dog is in the Details
9. Dog Knows
10. Dog's Green Earth
11. A Litter of Golden Mysteries
12. Dog Willing
13. Dog's Waiting Room
14. Dog's Honest Truth

Acknowledgments

My editor, Randall Klein, always makes these books better. I'm fortunate to have some great beta readers as well, including Judith Levitsky, Jim Bessey, Cindy Woods, K.J. Roberts, Bob Kman, Annette Mahon, and Nancy Ann Gazo. Thanks also for the terrific cover to Kelly Nichols.

I would like to acknowledge the support of my colleagues at Broward College, and my fellow members of Mystery Writers of America. And of course my husband Marc and our golden retrievers, Brody and Griffin, who continue to inspire me with their antics.

www.ingramcontent.com/pod-product-compliance
Lightning Source LLC
LaVergne TN
LVHW012016060526
838201LV00061B/4324